The Time Capsule Murders:

BOOK TWO

Dial Emma For Murder

Author Unknown

Presented by

Hamish De'Lamet & Chandral Ramon

PANGEA PUBLISHING
www.PangeaCorp.com

PUBLISHING
www.PangeaCorp.com

First Edition PANGEA Publishing edition April 2013
© 2009 by the Schulte Brothers, Hamish De'Lamet & Chandral Ramon

Published by PANGEA.
ISBN-13: 978-0-9894065-0-5 (PANGEA Publishing)
ISBN-10: 0989406504

Visit the Web Site: www.TimeCapsuleMurders.com

Dedicated to our agent, Alphonse van Worden, Chandra's Dad Chuck, our mentors, Leo and John Schulte, the Good People of PANGEA, especially John C. Besmehn & Cheryl Ann Wong. For Blythe Abigail Su-Ren Schulte -- thanks for your inspiration and for coincidentally falling into our reading demographic!

Dial Emma For Murder

Introduction

This is the second journal that we found in the box – we being Hamish and Chandral. We wished we hadn't found it, of course, because it meant that the nightmare kept on going! In the introduction to Book One, we wrote that we could sleep at night, only if we assumed that this was all fiction, which we are still not sure about! And now Book Two has made it even harder for us to sleep at night!

Chandral had a recurring nightmare that came back to her for weeks, after we finished putting Book Two of the story together from this journal. She kept seeing a staircase and a pair of scissors and a dark liquid circling around a drain. And then she thought she saw Anna, the girl found dead in the school bathroom at the end of *Why Begins With W*. Or at least she saw a girl that her imagination dreamed up as Anna. In Chandral's nightmare Anna moved up the staircase with the scissors in her hand, and in the dark at the top of the stairs was this drain, in the ceiling, with something black running into the drain. And as she climbed closer to the top, the ceiling and stairs began to converge and suffocate her! Chandral blamed it all on this book. I told her not to worry, because the story in the Time Capsule cannot be real. At least, that was my feeling at the time. (The result has been that I have had to take over and do most of the heavy lifting in editing: Chandral needed a break!)

And yet…we both knew that the story **could** be a fact! We might not want to believe it, we might want to deny it, but the truth remains the truth. Our opinions about it will make no difference. You can believe that a table is a lamp: the table will not care. It will stay a table! And no matter how many times you go to turn the table on, no light will shine. And so, who can know if these manuscripts tell the truth or not? Our agent has hired a detective, much like the narrator does in this book, to investigate unsolved crimes which might fit the events told here. But we told him that was the wrong way to look at this situation: any investigation needs to look at **solved** crimes! That was the problem! The narrator, whoever he or she was, or still is, wrote that the police consider everything solved! But our publisher insists on digging deeper and has encouraged our agent to keep searching for more evidence. If these journals prove to be real, then the value of these manuscripts is likely to soar!

-- Hamish De'Lamet & Chandral Ramon

Lynchburg, 2010

October 2

Anna died 3 weeks ago, and here is what I remember the most. The school again went through a depression, and was closed down for a day of mourning. Again absenteeism went up, and again the administration brought in extra counselors to help classmates and friends of Anna make it through their thoughts and memories. And I remember the newspaper articles and the television news shows clucking about how they had predicted something like this! "Clusters" was the main word: "cluster suicides" were typical in cases like this. A trauma like Aura Malper's murder was almost guaranteed to cause at least one suicide among weak-minded teenagers. And no, the suicidal teenager did not need to know the deceased. The cluster syndrome was well-researched. The vidiots (that's an idiot on a video screen) proudly predicted more deaths to come, despite the counseling "interventions" taking place at the school. Of course, ace T.V. reporter Buffy Blondebrain did hope her prediction would not come true! But parents were now hereby warned by Television News, the New Mother of America!

The police said Anna died either of an accidental drug overdose, or a deliberate overdose for suicide. The drugs belonged to Anna's mother: the bottle was found next to Anna in the school bathroom. Buffy's cousin on another station, Blondie Bubblebrain, actually shook her finger at the camera and scolded parents for not keeping their prescription drugs locked up "to protect the children." She then slammed a medicine cabinet shut and padlocked it. Great television drama! Or maybe it was really meant to show the drooling audience at home how to protect their children from legal prescription drugs.

America loves to be scolded for not being perfect. It's almost as much of a national sport as baseball or football. America is scolded for not doing more for the children, for not making every moment safe and worry-free. And so America spoils its already very spoiled children: the television sets pour out guilt, and the guilt sends the parents to empty their bank accounts on their children. This is called "stimulating the economy," and America depends on the cycle to keep millions of hard-working people employed... in China.

What else caused Anna's death, asked the media, besides careless parents? Depression, the newest contagious disease hitting teenagers everywhere! Maybe it was depression over Aura Malper's murder, said the media morons. Maybe a legal dose of Prozac would have helped her fight the depression. Or okay, maybe she took the drugs just to get high, just for a thrill. Maybe she was not depressed after all. Maybe this and maybe that.

The truth: yes, Anna was depressed. But I'll add one more "maybe" to the list.

Maybe Anna was murdered.

By a serial killer.

The serial killer who murdered our school's head janitor, Richard Laurenz, and junior Aura Malper. The serial killer who whispered in Anna's ear to stay silent when she was semi-conscious on the floor. The serial killer working in our school as the #2 janitor, although now he seems to be #1 thanks to the demise of Mr. Laurenz.

If I was positive on September 10th that "Uncle Al" the janitor was the murderer of Aura and Mr. Laurenz, I had to admit that at first I was not quite so positive that he had directly murdered Anna. Forcing pills down a person's throat should have left some sort of evidence. The police should have found marks on her throat, bruises, something to indicate an attack. Fact: Anna confessed to me that she was stealing and popping her mother's pills. She was trying to forget everything she had seen that day near the janitor's office, trying to forget that threatening voice with the bad grammar: *Don't tell nobody nothin'!* So it was possible that the official explanation of accidental overdose/suicide was correct.

Except for one thing, which more and more gnawed at me. Near the end of the newspaper story there was a detail thrown out, as if it meant little. "A mark on the victim's head was consistent with a small bloody mark on the edge of the toilet, where the victim hit her head after fainting."

The police cannot be that stupid. This city is big enough to have detectives who know better than that. Would anybody go into a bathroom stall and start taking pills *while standing up?* Anna would have sat down on the seat: she was tall enough to be seen standing in the stall. That led to another problem: why would she bother going into a bathroom stall late after school to pop pills? The place was deserted: she could have just gone to a water fountain. And anyway, would she have fainted that quickly?

On the other hand, who knows? Yes, Anna *could* have gone into the bathroom for her pill thrill, just to be sure nobody would see her. Yes, she *could* have gone into the stall and not sat down. People in suicidal moods, or under the influence of drugs, are not examples of logical thinking. Yes, this was the most obvious solution.

Except for another thing, which also gnawed at me more and more. Anna had promised me that she was stopping the drug use. Yes, I know it's near the end of the 20th century, and people rarely keep promises. Me-first-ism is the main philosophy: just watch people driving on the streets and highways as proof for that. I might only be 14, but I'm not blind to attitudes in America today. Here's one of the main ideas in Me-first-ism: if my life becomes easier suddenly by breaking a promise to you, well, you'll just have to understand that a promise really doesn't mean anything these days! Why would you really expect me to keep my word? This isn't the 19th century any longer with its obsolete morals! Get with the program! Therefore, if Anna said she would keep her head straight, so that she could find the courage to go to the police and finally tell them her story, how much was that promise worth these days?

Still, I saw Anna's face when she made that promise. I believe she meant it.

So Anna's promise and the detail about how she hit her head on the toilet combined in my brain to form a different death scene: Uncle Al the janitor spotted her with me on September 9th, the day we went to the closet where Aura's body was found. He began to get nervous about what we were doing, and looked for an opportunity to eliminate Anna, the semi-witness to his crime of hanging Mr. Laurenz. Of course, it's also possible he had always been looking for an opportunity to kill her, and preserve his (so far) perfect crime.

So somehow he follows Anna, or sees her go into that bathroom, and takes the chance that nobody else is around. I can't explain how he knew about her drug use. No, he could not have known: maybe he was going to fake her suicide by hanging, like he did with Mr. Laurenz. But then he sees her gulping down a pill or two at the sink, or maybe she was at the water fountain taking a pill, and that was the opening he needed. He grabs her and covers her mouth with his gloved hand, gets her into the bathroom stall, and knocks her out on the toilet edge. Then he finds the pills in her bookbag, and he is amazed at his good luck! Two bottles! He puts the pills into her mouth, a few at a time, massages her throat, maybe even forces a small cup of water down her to make her swallow. That might bring her back to consciousness, but by that time he's already put enough pills into her stomach for the fatal result.

Did I believe this?

It depends on the day. Sometimes it depends on the hour. If I buy the police versions, and ignore Anna's story and Sam's story and Emma Risley's absolute belief that her uncle had to be innocent of killing Aura, then my life is simple, uncomplicated, lacking in danger. Remember I got into all of this because I was bored with school back in August!

I'm not bored now.

Perhaps you want to know how I felt about Anna's death. How did I "handle" it? How did I "deal" with it? Those are interesting words we use in such situations: "handle" a death, as if it's something you can mold like clay, and "deal" with death, as if it's a card game, and the loser winds up with the Ace of Spades. I only knew Anna for about a month. She was nice, too nice, and because she was too nice she was too unsure about herself. That's why she never had the faith in herself to tell the police her story. And maybe because she doubted her own instincts, and couldn't believe her own eyes and ears, maybe because of that she was dead.

So how did I feel about Anna's death? I'm not spelling it out for you. Ask yourself how you'd feel! All I can say is: I didn't have too many witty things to say to anybody for a couple of days. My mother was quietly watching me, which is what you'd expect from somebody who followed the T.V. news every night. When she asked me if I happened to know Anna, my shrug and the words "sort of" allowed her to show concern and sympathy. My father wanted to know how "the other kids" were doing at school during this time of crisis, but "the other kids" was a code for "you" of course. They then openly wondered if I shouldn't just stay home to return to our home-schooling routine, or maybe they should transfer me to another school, a private school, devoid of murder and suicide. The media reported that there were more than several students transferring away. Perhaps I should be one of them? No, I said, I'm fine. Things will be fine.

So what did I believe? If Uncle Al is a premeditating killer, then I can't explain how he knows that Anna was stealing her mother's pills, so that he can fake her overdose. It could be that he did premeditate her murder, and, like I said, just got lucky with the pills. On the other hand, a quick, unprepared murder might be a new thrill for him.

No matter what I believed about the "how," it was irrelevant: there was one unpleasant fact hanging over me, so to speak.

Uncle Al knows I was with Anna, near the site of Aura's murder.

Uncle Al snarled at me with a triple negative the day before Anna died.

Uncle Al might want me dead.

October 3

In English Anna's desk is still empty. On the first day of class after her death some of the kids thought her desk should be removed. Several of the girls protested, and even some of the boys agreed: removing the desk would be like saying Anna never existed. They wanted to remember her, even if it brought sadness at first.

A girl put a teddy bear on Anna's desk: the toy had a green ribbon around its neck. It formed a fancy bow in front. The girl was going to place it at the memorial for Anna on the front lawn, but decided this would prevent the desk from disappearing. She was right. The bear stayed at the desk for a few days, until one of the boys undid the ribbon and noosed the bear from the back of the chair: "Look! It's Mr. Laurenz!" he giggled, and the citizens of Dummydom in the room laughed and laughed, although most of the girls were horrified. You would expect an adolescent boy to do something like that. No girl could ever think of something so crude. An adolescent girl might write a dark, depressing poem about nothingness: the poem would counterbalance her feelings about the loss. But there are too many boys who would lynch a toy bear to hide their feelings about the same loss.

I stood up and returned the bear to its natural condition.

"You're a moron," I said to the hangman, "and that's an insult to real morons."

He wasn't sure what the last part meant, but had enough electricity in the cauliflower he used as a brain to understand the first 3 words.

"Just a joke, loser. Why's it your business?"

"Stopping morons is always my business," I said with a smile. The smile confused him, maybe because he really was a moron.

"Always better 'n' smarter than everybody else, ain'tcha?"

"No, but I'll always be better and smarter than you."

This led to delighted cackles from the hens, and the other roosters crowed remarks at the moron like "You're fried!" or "You are so burned!"

"You're just a loser, and the narc, and everyone knows it!"

And the chicken coop was filled with cries of Whoa!

"Really? If I'm the narc, then you'd better be careful. How much would you pay for me *not* to slip a bag of weed into your locker and then call my friends, Mary and Jane, the drug dogs?"

"Is that some sort of threat? I've got witnesses here," he said cockily.

"You might have witnesses, but you have no wit. You just proved that I'm not the narc, and you don't even know it! The next time you get into a battle of wits, make sure your opponents are named Dim, Nit, or Half. They'd be more on your level."

The appearance of Mr. Randolph ended the debate, and he sensed the tension in the room and the anger in the moron. Since I was still standing by Anna's desk with the stuffed bear, he was not sure what to say.

"Is there a problem in here?" he asked finally.

"Just fixing Beau Bear's bowtie," I said. "It was causing him some discomfort: he said it was choking him." This evoked more giggles and snorts, and Mr. Randolph's face acquired the teacher expression called I Know There's Something Going On.

This is one way teenagers "deal with death" of course: make rude, crude jokes about it. Why some teenagers get obsessed with death and dying is something of a mystery. Part of it comes from wanting to seem adult, so The Ultimate Question dominates their landscape. Part of it comes from that feeling of Immortality, which the hormone surge is causing: I'm so alive and full of sexual power, I can't die! Or at least not for a very long time! So I can do anything I want, no matter how stupid or dangerous! This belief is often disrupted by telephone poles or trees, which the believer has kissed at 90 miles per hour in his car.

Yes, Anna was not quite a friend, at least not in my definition of the word. I cared about her, and she probably felt closer to me than I did to her. I'll admit to not sleeping at all that first night, when the late night news announced her death. *She should've gone to the police* kept rotating in my head. And when that faded away, I just felt empty: those death poems by teenage girls come from the same experience.

No, that's not a clue as to whether I'm a boy or girl. You'll have to keep guessing.

And here's something else for you: all of these deaths suddenly seemed to revolve around me. There was a game of Good Versus Evil being played out, and ol' Dick Laurenz, Aura Malper, and now Anna were casualties of this game, a game played just for me and just with me. I was being tested for some reason, and 3 people were dead now, sacrificed for my... my what? Benefit? Education? Moral Development? Sure: this is just my good ol' Arrogance talking again. Arrogant, self-centered people always think things are happening around them for their own benefit. Or for their destruction: that's the road to paranoia.

So to avoid being the center of attention, let's talk about you. I guess I should wonder who you are. I haven't done that yet. I started this journal, now in a second notebook, out of boredom. And I wanted to wonder about the events at school in an organized way. I thought it would help me with solving this "mind-messing mystery" as I called it. In one sense you are me, or should I say "you are I" to be grammatically perfect. But some times grammatical perfection is wrong!

So maybe you are not me. But maybe nobody will ever be you, the reader of my words. And here I sit, writing a journal with short sentences for a reader who probably won't ever care. I ought to go back to my florid and dramatic style with a sentence like: *Perhaps I shall consign these scraps of papyrus to the flames and ashify their mysterious purpose forever!* How florid and dramatic would that be? Note how "ashify" is emphasized by the natural music in the words. No, I guess I'll keep my promise and write very simply. I'll probably just bury this story somewhere. I don't really think I'll ashify it. I know: you can't find "ashify" in your dictionary. I just made it up: but you should be able to puzzle it out and realize it means "turn into ashes." (The future might not be able to read very well. I hope you're not insulted, if you are in the future.) If you can read very well, good for you. No, you'll have to guess which year I'm living in. You already have enough clues. And if you were snooping around and found these journals, and have read them up to this point, then you must have a curious mind. That's good! Curiosity keeps you alive. It gives you strength.

So you are curious, possibly a good reader, and you live in the future. Are there bases on the Moon or Mars yet, like in science fiction? I actually don't like science fiction much: I like Westerns. I know: the Western isn't big like it used to be. Its morality usually isn't warm and fuzzy enough to include relativism, where morality equals immorality, and everything seems complex, when it is really just wrong.

I'm stalling you. I'm trying to avoid telling you about the second sleepless night, and how out of simple exhaustion my body forced itself to sleep on the third night after Anna's death. I also don't want to tell you about a second reason of why I was scared. It's possible that my imagination is creating all these problems, and that everything has happened according to the simple police explanation: Richard Laurenz stalked Aura Malper, killed her, and then committed suicide. Anna died a month later because she was using drugs. I'll admit that this scared me because of my pride: could my imagination be tricking my intelligence? I was always too cool and ironic and distant to be tricked into taking anything very seriously: I own the aquarium and I tap on the glass! I'm not in the aquarium and swimming around with the goldfish.

Simplest solution: they weren't victims of a serial killer, because there is no serial killer. That theory's just me, putting things together in the wrong way. But something told me I was right: Anna's face, Sam's face, Emma's face, and especially the face of Uncle Al the Janitor. Those faces told me I wasn't imagining everything. And so, it didn't matter whether Anna was a friend in any definition: I had to do something because it was the right thing to do. I had to take Anna's story to the police myself.

So on the day before Anna's funeral I rode the bus to the police station. Our suburb has a nice new building filled with Deputy Dawgs waddling around. To be fair, some of the policemen were in good shape. But the filled ashtrays by the entrance told me that I could probably outrun them all, fat or thin.

I told the receptionist that I'd like to talk to the officer who investigated the Aura Malper murder at my school. There was a pause.

"I don't understand."

"Can you find out who investigated the Aura Malper case?" I asked.

"Are you here to report a crime?" she asked robotically.

"Yes."

"Please have a seat on the right."

A robot might've had better information. There weren't many people around: this suburb didn't have much crime really, because most of the people had enough money. The poorest section was the area where Sam lived, and although it was part of a township and not the suburb, the poor kids went to the suburban school. They were the ones blamed for the drug dealing and abuse. But who had the most money to fool around with smack, crack, and slop?

I waited. Magazines, torn and ancient, were stacked up on a table next to the bench. Finally a policewoman chewing gum and waggling a clipboard came up to me.

"Yew wanted to re-port a cram?"

She was not born in this area.

"Report a crime, yes. Or, actually, I have some new information about an old crime."

"Widge izzit? Yew re-portin' a cram or not?"

"I have information about the Richard Laurenz and Aura Malper murder-suicide that happened at the high school in August."

I tried to sound as official and important as a 14-year old could. The policewoman stared at me and said:

"That's closed."

"Maybe it shouldn't be."

"Looky here: if yew file a o-fficial re-port, an' yew ain't tellin' the truth, yew all do now re-a-laz that kin be a cram tew?"

"Why would I not tell the truth?"

"Yew'd know better 'n' me."

"What I want to tell you also concerns the girl who died of the drug overdose at the school."

"That's closed tew. They got her funeral goin' on t'morrah."

"Maybe her case shouldn't be closed either."

"Hmph."

She left and went into an office where another policewoman was sitting at a computer. Exactly what we thought: the police wouldn't be interested in opening up a closed case. Of course Anna was more afraid that Uncle Al would know about her visit. What an irony: she never told the police anything, but died anyway.

But she had told me, and that broke the murderer's rule to her about keeping quiet. I was now looking at two policewomen coming toward me. I stood up: we were all the same height. One of the new ladies took care of the introductions.

"Did you investigate the murder-suicide at the high school?" I asked.

"No, but what's all this about? I don't understand."

So I gave them Anna's story, but without my suspicion of Uncle Al and without Sam's weaker, semi-earwitness account. I noticed while I was talking that their badges said "Victim's Services" in small letters. They nodded now and then and looked very serious.

"Now let me get this straight. This Anna, this is the same girl that died of the drug overdose?"

"Yes, and the threat from the real murderer caused her to use sleeping pills: she was usually in a nervous state," I explained.

"Anna was a good friend of yours, wasn't she?" asked the one who had so far stayed silent. I saw the name "Motes" on her badge.

"Actually, no. We were just in the same English class. She came to me because she thought I could help her."

"Help her how?" asked the first one, and when she frowned many wrinkles appeared on her forehead. Her badge seemed to say DiRafy: it was difficult to read. The name matched her dark hair and eyes.

"Help her by finding a way to catch the murderer who threatened her."

"Didn't your friend get any counseling at the school back in August to help her deal with her shock?"

"Sure, but it didn't seem to help. She couldn't get that voice and death out of her head. That's why she was on her mother's pills, to forget and get some sleep."

"But you seem to be pretty smart: you didn't think there was something wrong with her story?" asked Officer Motes.

"Yes, at first, but I also think there could be an alternate explanation."

"And what might that be?"

"That there was a third person present, who killed Aura and murdered Mr. Laurenz by faking his suicide."

"The evidence doesn't show that. And that's why the case is closed. Look, the investigators involved know all sorts of things about the case that you don't. I'm gonna ask you to trust them. They're professionals. We're sorry about your friend Anna, but, you know, the mind can do strange things. I don't know why your friend took drugs, but it wasn't because of what happened. And, you know, life goes on." Her voice became very quiet. "We know you don't want your friend to leave you, and you don't want her to leave you because of an accident with drugs maybe, but that's just the way it is."

So that's how I told Anna's story for her: the women promised that they would "mention" what I had told them to the investigating officers. But I really didn't want to file an official police report, now did I? It'll be good enough if she just tells the investigators what I said. Yeah, right, and we know what that means.

I can't write any more just now. Maybe tomorrow I'll ink my memories of the funeral.

October 4

They closed school for Anna's funeral. The family did not have a visitation at a funeral home. I was interested in watching for one person: Uncle Al, my murder suspect. I arrived at the church early to examine the mourners. Even though they could have just stayed home and slept, it seemed that most of the school was showing up. They could not have known Anna personally, and yet here they were, from freshmen to seniors, at a 9:00 A.M. Anglican funeral.

There is still hope for America!

The church became jammed, and my plan to watch for Uncle Al became a joke. It was now impossible to watch the 3 entrances because of all the people standing outside and chatting.

And then Sam showed up.

"Where've you been?" he asked.

"Nowhere."

There was a long pause.

"Do you think she really committed suicide?" he whispered.

"I don't know what I think," I said. Actually I did know, but I wasn't telling Sam right now. He was twitchy and squinting and sniffing constantly. His feet did a kind of Irish jig, up and down, up and down. For a few long moments he just looked around at the crowd.

"This is just so weird, y' know?"

"Yeah. Teenagers should not be buried."

There was another long pause. Sam smiled at me slightly, and then nervously shrugged his shoulders. A question was caught in his throat, and he needed me to perform the Heimlich Maneuver to get it out.

"Yes? Go ahead, say it, Sam. What's wrong?"

"She was your witness, wasn't she?"

This question wrecked me inside. I promised myself I wasn't going to cry. I had to clench my teeth, close my eyes, and stare down at the ground, before I could choke out my answer. And none of that identifies me as male or female.

"Yes."

Sam looked around, and bent down closer to me.

"You don't think she committed suicide at all!" he whispered.

"I told you already: I don't know what I think."

"You think she was murdered, just like the others!"

"It doesn't matter what I think. Here's what I know for certain: she was on drugs, different kinds of pills, the kind that can stop your heart if you take too many or mix them the wrong way. That's probably what happened."

"But you don't believe it."

I didn't respond at first.

"There's no evidence of anything!"

"What about what I heard?" he pleaded.

"What you heard on that day has all kinds of simple explanations. We've just been putting things together the wrong way and have a wrong answer. The case is closed and the police are right."

"But you don't believe they're right. You keep telling yourself that, but Anna was your witness. I thought the same thing when I heard about her death on T.V. The murderer did it, faked another suicide, like he faked suicide for Mr. Laurenz. That's the first thing I thought, and so did you."

"It's…not impossible, but we have absolutely nothing now."

"What about Anna's story?"

"Without Anna there is no story!"

The situation was splitting me into pieces: I really did want to mourn Anna, and I wanted to help Sam, but I needed to stay focused. And right now Sam was distracting me from spotting Uncle Al. I walked away and up the steps to get a better view. The hearse and the black limousines pulled up, and the crowd began to part automatically. Since anybody standing outside right now would be standing inside later, I walked into the filled church and looked for the steps to the choir loft. Sam followed me.

"I didn't know you were in the chorus," he said.

"I'm not, but I am today."

"Uh, maybe I shouldn't come with you."

"Why not?"

"I can't really sing."

"Then you'll fit right in."

I thought I could get a better look from a bird's-eye view. Uncle Al, unless he was disguised somehow, should be easy to find. It wasn't clear to me what it would mean if he showed up or not. I had picked up some books about serial killers at the library, but hadn't read everything in them yet. I knew to ignore practically everything in movies, television, and the press about how the F.B.I. or the local police handle profiling. These were books by professionals who often used words like "ludicrous" or "outlandish" to describe how pop kulcher portrays them. What I did know from my reading was this: different types of serial killers exist, and one type is highly organized. That kind gets a thrill from tricking the police and playing games with them.

Showing up at your victim's funeral is one of those games.

We picked up hymnals and stood on the edge of the chorus. The director, a man with an unfortunate last name, Mr. Muscat, didn't notice that his group had grown suddenly. There were a few blind spots where I couldn't see anybody. So far, no Uncle Al. But I did see Lana Todd and her group of blonde broom-pushers. I remembered them calling Uncle Al a really "cool guy." Even if he wasn't a killer, Uncle Al wasn't cool or hot or anything similar. Uncle Al was a first-class dweeb.

It turned out that this was no actual funeral. This was a "memorial prayer service." I heard later that Anna's parents just wanted something simple. So the Anglican priest delivered simplicity: a few readings from the Bible, from the Old and New Testaments, a few hymns from us in the chorus and the congregation, a short sermon full of clichés, and then a few more hymns and prayers and readings. Less than 30 minutes total.

The worst part was at the end. We sang the hymn *Going Home* with the famous melody by Dvorak from his Ninth Symphony. It was so sad, and so appropriate. The sniffling became widespread, and even some of the boys were wiping their eyes. A few girls downstairs stood up and left early. I looked over at Sam, and his face was red and wet.

"They sang that at my mother's funeral," he whispered, trying to excuse his lack of macho toughness. The information explained many things about Sam and his home situation. It might also explain why his father escaped from the house on those long trips in his truck. The bell in the tower started ringing slowly. Holy water was sprinkled over the casket. I tried not to think about Anna being inside of it.

We walked outside, and Sam stayed with me. My cousin Martika and Steve Cadosia spotted me. Sam took a step away, as if he were about to leave. Martika looked at Sam with moderate interest, when he took a few more steps away, but Steve just nodded at me with a sorrowful face.

"Can't believe we were just talking to her a couple days ago!" he said to me.

I just nodded and squinted toward the hearse.

"You didn't return my calls," said Martika. That was true: she had called the house a few times the day after Anna's death. I'm not sure I can say why I didn't call her back. Perhaps it was still too early then for me to say anything about Anna to anybody.

"There isn't much to say."

"I don't believe that, especially from you."

"Anna was on drugs, just like the police said. She admitted it to me, taking her mother's pills, just like the police said. That's probably where her story came from anyway: drug fantasy. And now, her death is just a warning to us all."

Martika squinted at me and said: "You think you can fool us now? The first thing I thought of was that guy, the one that whispered in her ear. He probably killed her in the restroom. And it's the first thing you thought of too!"

"Clever girl!"

Steve Cadosia wasn't sure what my words and attitude meant right now.

"So, uh, you gonna do anything about this?"

"No. The police said the case is closed."

"You went to them?" asked Martika with some nervousness, and so I gave her the one-sentence version of my dealings with the lawwomen. Sam was still hovering around the edge of the conversation, and both Martika and Steve looked at him, but with no recognition.

"This is our school's Master Sweeper, Honor Student, and Keeper of the Keys," I said, and everyone nodded.

"Keeper of the keys?" repeated Steve.

"You must be involved in this too," stated Martika.

"In what?" asked Sam, genuinely not sure what she was talking about.

"No, he isn't involved in anything," I said quickly.

Sam wasn't sure what to say now.

"Like I said, there's nothing to be involved in, except a sick girl's fantasies," and I started to walk away.

"What are you gonna do?" asked Steve.

"Nothing," I said and took a few more steps toward the hearse.

"We don't believe that!" said Martika.

Behind the hearse there was a delay while the cars were organized for the drive to the cemetery. The crowd dispersed slowly, but many people still milled around on the lawn and talked. Martika and Steve headed for the parking lot.

"Why am I the 'Keeper of the Keys'?" asked Sam.

"Do you have keys in your pocket?"

"Well, yeah."

"That's why."

My eyes zeroed in on Lana talking to a man whom I didn't recognize, until I looked more carefully.

She was talking to a clean-shaven man.

She was talking to Uncle Al, who had shaved off his moustache and long sideburns. He also had a shorter haircut. I had overlooked him because of his changed appearance. So he was here, just like I thought. Lana waved to Uncle Al and walked away with an odd look on her face: this had happened before with Lana. Most of the time she has a face that sings the song of the Scarecrow from *The Wizard of Oz*. But now and then she seemed sharp and above everyone around her.

"See what kind of car that guy drives," I asked Sam.

"Who is he?" and he squinted into the morning sun.

"Your boss."

"That's Al?"

"Yes, now go see what kind of car he drives."

"You're sure that's him?"

"Trust me: it's him. He's cleaned up for the funeral today."

"But why do you need to know what he drives?"

"Because I do. I'll tell you why later," and I walked off to intercept Lana.

Lana was staring into her purse. I pulled out some tissues.

"Need some?" I asked.

"No, it's okay, thanks," and she pulled out some hand sanitizer and rubbed her palms and fingers with it.

"Did you shake hands with Uncle Al over there or something?"

"You are so mean sometimes."

"Uncle Al's the mean one, I'd think."

"I'm sure I don't know what you mean."

"What did he say just now?"

Lana's face looked almost insulted.

"None o' your beeswax."

I couldn't believe my ears: my grandma would've heard that line when she was a kid.

"Sorry, I don't have hives because I'm not allergic to anything."

"Like, that is such a lame joke!" and she rolled her eyes.

"If it's lame, maybe it can get a welfare check. But c'mon: what were you talking about? Anything about Anna?"

"No, he just said, like, you know, see you tomorrow at school."

That made no sense. You don't go up to somebody and expect them to say "see you tomorrow." Lana had talked with him more than that anyway. I was wondering something about Lana. It made me queasy, like eating chocolate-covered fish. Lana was nice and just a little stupid. That's a dangerous combination. Because if she really was as dull and nice as she seemed, she was the perfect girl for Uncle Al to pick for his next victim. I could see where she could fall in lust (I won't use the phrase "fall in love" here) with a guy like Uncle Al. Older man, but not too much older, telling Lana how "awesome" she is, maybe even "awesome to the extreme," a phrase heard around school more and more.

"Why'd he shave off his hillbilly sideburns and moustache?" I asked.

"Yeah, good question! Like, I always thought…"

"And why did he kill Anna?"

That blindsided Lana. But even better, for a few moments she showed that 100+ I.Q. Dull and nice Lana disappeared for the moment. She blinked fast and took a step away. Then she gulped down what was left in a large coffee cup from a fast-food factory. I could tell she was thinking extreme thoughts about what to say. Her face became older looking with deeper frown lines, and the crinkles by her eyes lengthened. I probably shouldn't've said it: but I wanted to shake Lana up for her own good. And what if Lana isn't stupid at all? I remembered that day when I punched out the two druggies, and Lana happened to come by with that different 100+ I.Q. personality. It didn't last long, but she seemed more natural when she seemed smart.

So if the sugar and caffeine washing through her brain had left any intelligence behind, I wanted to keep it from drowning.

"Why would you say something like that?" she asked.

"Because I think the odds are better than 50-50 that it's true."

"But why?"

"Because he's a model sleazeball, even without his sleazy moustache and haircut. I don't trust him."

"I thought you knew something specific," and that last word revealed the other smarter Lana, who hid behind a mask of bad mascara and discount make-up.

"I might, but right now let's just say if I don't trust him, you shouldn't either."

"What're you mixed up in?" and she whispered now, even though the crowd on the lawn was pretty thin, and nobody could have heard her.

"I might ask you the same thing."

A cliché of course, but my words again caught her off guard just a little.

"That isn't an answer."

Interesting: this Lana uses the more intelligent sounding contraction "isn't," but Lana Lazybrain would've said "That's not…" and smeared the s into the not.

"I agree, but I think you and your friends on the work crew need to be careful around Uncle Al."

Suddenly Lana Lazybrain made an entrance.

"Like, you are so unfair! I don't know, like, what to say, it's just so unfair!"

"And mean too, right?"

"Well…yeaaah!" and she sing-songed the vowels extravagantly in outrage.

Sam was marching back from the parking lot.

"Here comes Sam. He's going to tell me that Uncle Al drives a van, probably an old Chevy van."

Lana again alternated in her expressions between intelligent speculation and deep dumbness. Sam nodded and said "Hi" to Lana. Then he said:

"He drives a big van."

I looked slyly at Lana.

"An old one probably, from the 70's or early 80's?" I asked.

"I don't know about that, but it was kind of rusty on the edges."

"No windows on the sides, right?"

"Yeah, how'd you know? And the back windows had Megadeth and Black Sabbath sunblockers on them."

"I would've expected something from a rockabilly band," I said.

"So what's it mean? What difference does it make if he drives a van?"

"I'll have to think about it some more."

Lana was spotted by her friends, and they came over to us. Lana then said:

"You're wrong about Al. He's a really nice guy, and if you don't think so, you should just stay away from him and keep your opinions to yourself," and she left with her group. Then she stopped and said: "Just stay away from him all the time!"

"What's she mean? Why are you wrong about Al? And why should you stay away from him?" asked Sam.

"I called him a sleazeball and she got upset."

"Yeah, I guess he is kind of a sleazeball."

"See? You know I'm not wrong about Al."

"So, c'mon, what about his van? What's up with that?"

Large vans with no side or rear windows so you can't see inside too well: all the better to hide what I'm doing, my dear. Uncle Al might need a van like that some day. Or he might have already needed it, and used it, for a murderous purpose. Was I being too imaginative? Was I being mean and unfair? It didn't matter: I had no physical evidence about anything in this case! So why not theorize and accuse a technically innocent man of 3 murders?

But I didn't want to upset Sam too much with my theory.

"I'll tell you later, like I said."

"Well, so now what?" he asked.

"Go back home, I guess."

"Why don't you come over to my place?"

And now you're sure this invitation will reveal my gender! If I refuse, you'll think it's absolutely because I'm a girl, and that I don't want to be alone with a boy 2 years older. And therefore if I accept, I have to be a guy. But you've forgotten that nobody scares me, especially not Sam. I could cripple him at the elbow or the knee, or both, if necessary. We all know Sam better than that anyway.

"My dad's home. He'll be sleeping 'cause he got in late last night, but if we're quiet, it'll be okay."

"So what's happening at your place? Why the invitation?"

Sam looked uncomfortable and guilty. He looked at the grass and its collection of orange and brown leaves.

"There's something I got to show you."

"What is it?"

Again he looked like he had done something wrong.

"I just, I don't know what it is. It's a letter."

"What? Another threat from those dead-heads we beat up?"

"I don't know who it's from," and he hesitated. "I haven't opened it."

"So are you thinking it's from the dead-heads? Why should you worry about any of them? We can handle them."

"I think, I'm afraid, I think... I think it's from Anna."

Where was this suddenly coming from? I had basically kept my two witnesses apart to test any evidence. Anna knew only that there was a second witness in the area, who – maybe – heard the hanging of Mr. Laurenz along with the name "Kaplan" twice. She did not know Sam's name, and only today did Sam guess who Anna was.

So how could he have a letter from Anna, when they didn't know each other?

"Don't be afraid. It can't be from Anna."

"Why not?"

"Because I never told her your name, just like you didn't know about her. Safer that way, and keeps any evidence cleaner."

"I still have this feeling that it's from her."

"And why do you 'think' or 'feel' that it's from her? There's no return address?"

"No."

"And you never thought it could just be some junk mail?"

"No." He paused. "You must think I'm pathetic."

"No, I think you're stressed out because of the shock from the hanging, because of your responsibilities at home, because of all the normal stress of school, because of everything."

I also thought he was being superstitious, but I didn't tell him that.

"Okay, let's take a look at this mysterious letter."

Time's up: I've re-read everything, making sure this is exactly what happened. I probably should never have let so much time go by, before I started keeping track of this part of the case.

October 6

I couldn't write anything yesterday. My parents cruelly abducted and tortured me for hours: a shopping expedition to buy some winter clothes and new shoes. They haven't coped with the idea yet that I'm old enough to handle that without them. Just give me a few green pictures of Andrew Jackson and pick me up in 2 hours. You'd think they would like not having to deal with a moody, rather depressed teenager in the mall. But keeping me a child keeps them younger than they are. They don't want to admit the terrible ticking truth from every clock in the Universe. I'm becoming an adult, and they're approaching 40 years old, the magical Biblical number. But I smiled as much as I could and tolerated the experience.

And there was some homework to take care of, which lasted longer than usual: yes, even though it is a public school, and the standards and demands are a joke, I at least do write out Math exercises, and I read the crock-of-crap novels for English, and so on. If I didn't get top grades all the time, then I'd be a disgrace to myself, since I think the place is an educational sewer.

But today I'm writing down the basics of my visit to Sam's house, after the memorial service for Anna was over. I noticed three things immediately when we walked in: one was that Sam's little brother was home. His name is Josh, and he's 8 years old. I talked to him while Sam went into the kitchen, where his father was.

"Are you sick?" I asked.

"Nope!"

"So why are you home?" I knew the grade school was still in session. Their classes weren't cancelled for Anna's burial.

"My dad's home, so I get to stay home today!"

Another thing was that the air was filled with the aromas of bacon grease and tobacco smoke.

"You shouldn't be smoking at your age," I said to Josh, and blew away the cloud of cancer in the living room. "You should wait until you're 10 or 12 at least."

"I don't smoke," and Josh giggled. "That's my dad!" Then he added: "You're crazy!"

"Oh, not really. I'm just a little crazy, like people who voted twice for Clinton."

"Who's that?"

"A cheeseburger expert."

Josh laughed again, even though he could not have understood the humor. The other thing I had noticed was that the flat, terribly off-key voices of the Beatles were also polluting the air in the house.

"And why are you listening to the Beatles?"

"My dad's playing that!" and Josh giggled again.

"He is?" I whispered. "Doesn't he know they're overrated?"

"What's 'overrated' mean?"

"It means they suck lemons, and that's why they can't sing right."

Josh was giggling again when his father and Sam came into the room. The truck driver had a dish towel on his right shoulder and he put his hands on his hips. Since his hands stayed on his hips when Sam introduced me, I just smiled and nodded to him. Josh then laughingly told his father my musical observation that the Beatles suck lemons. He didn't laugh or respond. He was like Sam in that: I had never yet heard Sam laugh. And a smile was rare. Maybe that's just the way he is, or maybe it's the way he's become since seeing Mr. Laurenz hang from that pipe.

"They're just not my style," I explained quickly to avoid insulting him further. "Of course, rock music isn't supposed to be perfect musically. That's why it's got mass appeal. For the older stuff I might pick a group like Steppenwolf instead."

"Tastes change," he grunted. He was slightly shorter than Sam, and actually rather skinny. They had the same kind of oily black hair. Sam's height and large frame must have come from his mother.

"And anyway, Duke Ellington said there were only two kinds of music."

"Good 'n' bad, that's right. A kid like you knows about Duke Ellington, huh?"

"Sure, *Take the A Train* and all that jazz. My mom likes his stuff, and thought it should be part of my education."

"She did, huh?"

"She likes C.C.R. too. An American sound, like the Beach Boys, who are a little more on-key than some other groups. Of course, if you want a wild, raw sound, you might as well go all the way with Mitch Ryder and the Detroit Wheels."

No response. This made me nervous. I always became nervous and started talking too much around adults who were not well-educated. This was one reason why my public-school teachers probably thought I was arrogant.

"Then you have hybrid groups who aren't bad, like C.S.N.Y. Half of them are Americans. Of course they're still mixing in pacifist politics, which ruins things for me. In a war pacifists are the first losers. And just because Communism is gone in Russia doesn't mean there can't be a war again somewhere."

"Mmhm."

It was unclear if he didn't understand, or wasn't interested in the opinions of an arrogant 14-year-old teenager on rock-music history and politics.

This ended the conversation. Sam was standing next to him and looked anxious, the way teenagers always look when their parents and peers are together in the same room. Which generation will be the first to embarrass or annoy the other one?

Josh turned on the T.V. set, which made the house a multi-media event despite the Beatles asking in the kitchen that we *Let It Be.* Right then a T.V. station beamed an ad for their noon news.

"Look!" said Josh, as a picture of our school flashed on for 2 seconds, followed by a picture of the Anglican church. A reporter was standing alone on the lawn. "They're talkin' 'bout your school."

The girl reporter was jabbering and using all kinds of hand movements to fill the screen with action, and the camera zoomed in, showing the church and then panning around the lawn to make it seem like something was happening there now. But nothing was happening.

"That's right, Bill, we'll have the full report at noon of course, so stay tuned here at Action 17 News for all the latest developments on this tragic, tragic story. They just had the funeral a few moments ago" (her hand sweeps across the background) "at St. Matthew's Church, it's an Anglican church, and the entire area here" (again a big sweep of the hand with a few up and down motions, as if she were erasing a blackboard) "was filled with mourners for Anna Wallingford, her death the third death since August, another shock to the school community…"

Sam turned it off.

"It's interesting when people die, isn't it?" I remarked.

"Huh," and Sam's father went back into the kitchen. Josh made a declaration of the rights of a child to watch T.V. and turned it back on. Sam motioned to me that I should follow him down the hall to his room. He shared it with Josh. On the way I glanced into the other bedroom: there was a wedding picture on an old white dresser. I wanted to see what Sam's mother looked like, but couldn't really just barge in to see it more clearly. The bedroom also showed what's called a "woman's touch," with flowered draperies and a frilly bedspread.

An odd feeling struck me: there was something almost holy about the room. I couldn't explain this to myself. Maybe it was just the atmosphere of the church connecting to Sam's deceased mother. Just an hour ago we were part of that large crowd saying good-bye to Anna. The ceremony at the cemetery was probably over now. What used to be Anna would soon be placed in the ground, after everyone had left.

I chased away that thought by continuing the conversation about T.V. news.

"Anyway, give it another day or two," I said. "Somebody else will die, and they'll forget all about this 'third death since August' completely."

"The last time," said Sam, "the story was even on the national news."

"Yeah? So? It was the kind of story the news needs: teenage girl stalked and murdered by a perverted loser, who commits suicide."

"Mr. Laurenz wasn't a perverted loser."

"You know it and I know it," I explained, and also thought to myself that Emma definitely knew it too. "But they're not selling normalcy. Have you noticed normal people aren't on the news? They need a freak show."

Sam didn't seem to pay attention to my media criticism. He stared with a sour face at his room. Stacks of clothes, possibly clean, but probably dirty, formed a mountain chain from the floor to the desk and dresser. One stack barely allowed a stereo boombox to peer into the sunshine. Sam seemed to debate about something, and then picked up an envelope from a bedside table.

"This is it."

"And you have this psychic power telling you it's from Anna: where are those other notes you got from the dead-heads?"

"I threw 'em away."

"Too bad. We could've compared the handwriting. I kind of have a memory of what the handwriting looked like. So, let's see what we have here."

First I looked at the envelope, and noticed something wrong.

"The stamp isn't cancelled."

Sam said nothing. He shrugged and sat down on his bed.

"When did this come?"

"I don't know."

"Don't you check the mail every day?"

"No, Josh gets it. That's his big thrill. Little kids like that. We just pile it up for my dad. He goes through it when he comes home."

I was suspicious of course. True, sometimes the post office machines will miss an envelope, and it goes through without being cancelled. The other explanation was that somebody put a stamp on it, and then just shoved it into the mailbox here. But why would anybody do that? The address was in generic block letters, so any indication of gender was – as far as I knew – impossible to determine.

"It says 'Sam Worcester' on it."

"That's me."

"That's proof Anna could never have sent this. She didn't know anything about you. I never told her."

Sam's reaction again was indifferent, but then I thought the indifference was a mask for nervousness. It was an upsetting day, and had been an upsetting week. My own feelings were fried enough, and I'll admit to being a little cooler in the past days, even with fried feelings. See? Another silly joke to chase away the sadness.

"Do you want to open this now?" I asked.

"I don't know."

"That means 'no' in my opinion. But I can tell you that Anna never wrote this." I paused and added: "Hey, maybe it's from a girl who likes you!"

"Don't be stupid."

"Then maybe it's from a boy who likes you."

Sam smiled ever so slightly. Still, it was a kind of sad smile, the kind with too much effort and too many clouds waiting to chase it away.

"Now that's really stupid," he said.

"Last chance to give me a definite answer, yes or no. Do you want me to open this now?"

Josh came galloping down the hall.

"What's goin' on?" he asked.

"We're trying to figure out how to roast you," I said.

"You are not!" and he giggled again.

"If we slice him in half, we can get him into the oven that way," I suggested.

Josh ran away to tattle on us to his father. I opened the letter.

"Hey!" and Sam acted like he had changed his mind, but he didn't even attempt to grab the letter.

I squinted at everything first. It was not hand-written. A computer dot-matrix printer had produced it. The printer's cartridge must have been worn out, because the words were not very dark. The paper on the edge was perforated, so the paper was part of a roll.

"Well, if we were the F.B.I. or the police, we'd have a clue because…" and I flashed the letter to Sam, "you can identify individual printers."

Sam said nothing about this extremely brilliant observation.

"And of course," I continued, "there could be fingerprints."

"So what's it say?"

"Do you really want to know?"

"I want to know if it's from Anna."

"It isn't. Trust me about that."

I read the letter silently to myself. There wasn't much in it. And it was not from Anna.

"We know what happened in the restroom. Bring your friend there tomorrow at 3:00 after school and we'll tell you."

"So who's it from?" asked Sam.

"There's no signature. Nothing."

"Does it mean they saw Anna die?"

None of this was making any sense. Who could the "we" in the letter be? At least two people who were around when

Anna was taking pills, or being attacked and forced to take pills? Why would they come to us? Why wouldn't they just go to the police? Did somebody whisper a threat in their ears too? A more lethal interpretation was that Uncle Al somehow knew about Sam's connection to me, had perhaps noticed us when we had not noticed him. The letter and invitation could be bait.

No, it was much more likely that the threat was from the Nazi dead-head druggies. Sam already had received threats from them. The reference to the restroom was ambiguous: it could mean the restroom where I interrupted their drug party with Sam's help. It didn't have to mean the restroom where Anna was found dead. That was the simplest solution, which I was always looking for in this case.

"No, it's probably from the potheads," and I explained why.

"I had this feeling it was from Anna: I was really sure it was from her as soon as you admitted that she was the witness."

"Your feeling was wrong," and I tossed the letter onto his bed. He didn't look at it. "You know there's something else wrong about this."

Sam looked confused and also depressed. Did he really want the letter to be from Anna? Why? Why would he want a letter from a girl who was either murdered or committed suicide? It almost seemed that he would be happy now, if Anna had signed her name at the end.

"The whole letter is ridiculous," I continued. Sam now seemed upset. I didn't understand his reaction. "Why mail an invitation like this with no date? How could the reader ever know which day 'tomorrow' is supposed to be? There's no guarantee the mail would be delivered on an exact day, or that the reader would not let days go by before opening it. And that's just what happened."

"So, so now what? It means nothing?"

"Well, I'd say it means something. But it has nothing to do with the case."

I decided to leave, and told Sam I was expected at home for lunch. In the living room Josh and his father were watching Bugs Bunny cartoons. As I said good-bye I now noticed that a pillow and several blankets were stacked up between the edge of the couch and the wall. My eyes quickly measured the size of the couch, and I realized something rather sad. The best word for it is "melancholy" actually, a more complex sadness.

Their father slept on the couch, not in that bedroom.

October 12

I've deliberately let the case – if there is a case – just coast since I left Sam's house. If there is a murderer, especially if Uncle Al is the one, then it seems wise to let things calm down for a while. That doesn't mean I've done nothing. I've done all kinds of things. Today in World Geography Mr. Dunwoody was talking about Columbus Day, and why it was no holiday to celebrate for the American Indians, also known as Native Americans. He began to give politically correct nonsense about how North and South America were Gardens of Eden, until the white man came bringing slavery and disease and genocide. And all that started with Christopher Columbus.

It was time to strike a blow for the truth. I raised my hand. Mr. Dunwoody cautiously recognized me.

"Have you read the writings of Christopher Columbus?" I asked.

"Just some excerpts," he said with hesitation. I didn't believe him, but continued as if he were telling the truth.

"Then I don't understand how you can say he started genocide, when he praised the Indians as the most beautiful people on earth, and that they were morally superior to the Spaniards. He came to do business with them, not wipe them out. He always thought he was somewhere near India."

"But he paved the way for genocide with his so-called discovery."

"For the Europeans it was a discovery, and for the Native Americans too. Neither had any idea that the other existed."

Lana cleared her throat and raised her hand:

"Like, so, what about the Vikings? I thought they discovered America too."

Having Lana in the debate was like, you know, having an extra tenth of a brain on my side.

"That's true," said Mr. Dunwoody. "But their villages failed, and word didn't spread to the rest of Europe."

"Interesting that it's the Europeans knocking on the doors of America, and not the Aztecs or the Iroquois sailing down the Rhine or the Thames," I said.

"That isn't the point. The point is that the Europeans almost wipe out all the natives here."

"But mainly through the bad luck of disease. It wasn't deliberate. It wasn't genocide."

Now you understand why I can't let the case go: I have to know and keep the truth pure. For Mr. Dunwoody the truth was a myth, and he replaced it with his own myth, where Columbus is a maniac hoping to kill every Indian. You can call that a disease. My disease was that I won't stay silent when the truth is unknown, or distorted.

"Like, you're really something else today," Lana said to me after class.

"Just trying to stay focused," I said.

"Yeah?" and she acted puzzled, until she realized what I meant. Then very seriously she said: "Oh, yeah!"

Anna's death was different from the other two: I knew her personally, and her death was pushing me deeper and deeper into myself. I needed to "stay focused" on school and keep myself open.

Especially my mouth had to be open!

Take English class for example: every week one day is "Vocab Day." (The slang word "vocab" hurts my ears, but the teacher thinks he's communicating with his class better if he uses fewer syllables. He might be right.) We're supposed to make up sentences from a "New Vocab" list to prove we understand the word. And then we read our sentences out loud to be judged as to how well we understood the word.

You can imagine the results because of the lack of effort, interest, and creativity. My classmates offered shining vocab gems like *The paralegal is here. The discrimination is happening. And then there was my favorite: I can hear the conundrum.*

One week the list had a series of hyphenated words. Most would seem to be obvious in meaning, but they were not so obvious to the oblivious in the classroom. To entertain Mr. Randolph, our poor teacher, I offered a sentence for "heart-pounding."

"The *Old Man and the Sea* has as much heart-pounding excitement as the Book of Numbers," I said.

Reaction to this was zero. But Mr. Blandolph shook his head.

"You won't let it rest, will you?" he commented.

"I have another sentence for 'penny-pincher': The boss was a penny-pincher, until Penny sued him for sexual harassment."

The word "sexual" woke up most of the class, but the laughter and applause that followed mostly happened in my mind.

"Always with the puns," said Mr. Randolph, but this time he had smiled at least. "That's an old joke."

"Not for our generation," I smiled, and nodded back and forth to indicate the sleepy-eyed, down-and-out, videoized defenders of truth, justice, and the American way.

Mr. Randolph knew what I was doing, and I think he was grateful for it. I wanted to chase away the gloom that was hanging in the air. Nobody else would say it out loud, but Anna was still in the room: the shrine was turning into stone, like most of the students. No doubt the other courses where she was present were experiencing the same gloom. The counselors still offered their services, called "Sense of Loss Sessions" on the announcements, which was another phrase I hated. At the memorial service Anna's parents were drowned in the phrase "so sorry for your loss." I can't explain why I hate those words so much: perhaps because they're trite and heard on bad T.V. crime shows. Her parents were too polite: I think I would've grit my teeth and just stormed away. But people mean well at such times, even if their words are a cliché.

Another day bit the linoleum. After stopping at my locker I just looked around the hall. Kids left this school pretty quickly. Only the teams seemed to keep a small group around very long after the final bell. There was of course the very tiny group of motivated students like Emma Risley, who hung around the labs. I decided to find her. She was in the Biology lab again.

"Where've you been hiding? I've been wondering about you," she said.

"Probably you're wondering if I'm still looking into the case."

"Yeah, and I'm wondering something else."

"Don't tell me! I've become psychic in the last days. You want to know if I'm going to the football game, and if I'm not, you're going to invite me along. Sorry, I'm doing something really important: I'll be watching *Bowling For Dollars* on T.V. tonight."

Emma didn't laugh. Girls named Emma don't ever laugh. Or at least not much.

"I'm wondering if you're scared now."

Emma got right to the point. Dissection was her strongest talent.

"It depends on the day. On Tuesdays and Thursdays I'm not scared, because I'm positive the police story is correct. On Mondays, Wednesdays, and Fridays I'm afraid that everything we think about this case is real, that it isn't just imaginations baking in the oven too long."

"And on the weekends?"

"I'm ambivalent and even apathetic."

Emma continued her dissection and examination of the remains of a cat. She occasionally wrote notes in a massive binder.

"You're on your way to medical school, aren't you?" I asked.

"Right! And out of this punk town forever!"

"It isn't a bad punk town," I commented.

Emma cursed her life in our fair area with rude words. At that moment matching rude words, and much worse, were coming from down the hall. I left the lab and saw that there was a commotion at the Cave of the Heathers. This was actually a deep area under the stairs, where a good number of Heathers and Ambers and Tiffanys from the freshman class gathered during free times.

The commotion was a girl fight with the added attraction of a race card. One thing I hate about fights like this: the bystanders who just watch, instead of separating the fighters. The screamed obscenities echoed everywhere and the fight seemed to be brutal, but didn't involve red dripping corpuscles yet.

I pushed my way to the gladiatoresses and grabbed one. To my amazement Emma grabbed the other one. I didn't realize she had followed me. Two teachers were on their way, but the girls were still shrieking very vulgar venom. Although the echo in the stairwell made it hard to understand specific words, the insults were about their sexual capacities.

"What's this about?" asked one of the lady teachers.

"It seems to be a debate about her flux capacitor," I said.

Emma laughed! But nobody else did.

"Flux capacitor? That's not what I was hearing."

"Sure it was, just a little debate about time travel that seems to have gotten out of hand."

The two girls were now crying. You could tell these teachers really didn't want to be bothered with officially reporting a fight. The paperwork and other hassles involved were not worth it.

"Things've been… tense in this school because of… everything," I said confidentially. "I wouldn't push this any more." I wasn't making excuses for them. I really did think Anna's death, as well as the earlier deaths, were causing kids to act up and out more.

Like I said: I even saw it in myself.

"What's your name?" asked the other lady teacher.

I stated my official name: all 3 parts. (There is a fourth, but I'm not telling you or anyone that.) Then I introduced Emma. The teacher repeated our names and thanked us for showing responsibility.

"I'll take them into the restroom to get cleaned up," said Emma. This was fine with everyone since Emma was the oldest student here and is a take-charge kind of girl.

"What I really want to do is give a detention to all you girls here who just stood and watched these two tear into each other!" said the first teacher with growing anger. "They could've really hurt each other if these two Good Samaritans hadn't come by!"

Good for her! I thought to myself. She had a few more choice words, and then told everybody to go away. She didn't want them in her sight. This was met with grumbles of "not our fault" and "that's so unfair" and other typical excuses. But the teacher was right: and I caught the religious reference, too. That was interesting to hear in a public school!

The teachers then went to the restroom where Emma had taken the boxeresses.

"So what was it really about?" I asked one of the Ambers.

"God, it was just a joooke! Abby got all bent out of shaaape about iiit! She is sooo hyper about everythiiing, I just can't belieeeve iiit."

"What was the joke? Obviously it seemed funny to…the other girl."

"Oh God, it was aaall so stuuupid. Abby's, like, just looking in her mirror and tryyying to just kind of like comb her hair just right, and then, like, she goes like: 'God! I hate my hair! My bangs are bad.' And then Fatima laughs and goes: 'That's not what the football team says!' And then Abby just, like, started screeeaming and like, it all happened so faaast, you know? Abby went sooo nuts, and then Fatima goes nuts, and then like, you guys came up, sooo…"

Fatima: I'll have to remember her. Good joke!

Emma came out with the two freshmen. Then the teachers went into scolding mode for 30 seconds. Abby, the girl with reddish blond hair and nearly gray eyes, was very unsorry. As the teachers and Fatima left, I walked over to Emma, and thought we would just leave, when Abby says to me:

"I know you. I saw you talking to Anna now and then."

"Now and then, that's right."

"Anna was my friend. Maybe my best friend."

Suddenly I realized that I had seen Abby before in the halls. She had waved to Anna when we walked by. If they were best friends, then they must have known each other before coming here as freshmen.

"You went to grade school together?"

"Yeah, all 8 years. It's all been just so awful, ever since that day."

I looked at Emma and narrowed my eyes. Here was perhaps more information about Anna. Perhaps, just perhaps, Anna had told this best friend something that she would not tell me.

"Yeah, I know. We were in the same English class. Mr. Randolph's, last period. It's been weird in there without her."

"I don't know if I'll get over her dying."

"Suicide in a school bathroom," I said with incomprehension. "Or a drug overdose. I couldn't believe it."

"I *don't* believe it!"

I looked at Emma again and then asked: "Why not?"

"She wasn't *on* drugs! She didn't *do* drugs! Like, that just wasn't her!"

"What would you say if I told you that she was taking pills?"

"I wouldn't believe it!"

"Believe what you want: it's the truth. She told me about it."

"You? Like, why would she be telling you that? God! I'm her best friend! Why wouldn't she tell me?"

"Maybe she was embarrassed to admit it to you, because you were her best friend."

"No, not Anna, she's my best friend! She tells me, like, everything! I'd know if she's on drugs!"

"And I know she was on her mother's pills. She was having trouble calming down and sleeping. But she promised me she would stop taking them."

"God! This is like, so awful," and then Abby cursed and shook her head.

"Any idea why she thought she might need to take pills like that?"

"I don't know. She's pretty freaked out by that murder back in August, but everybody was freaked out."

"Yeah, tell me about it," mumbled Emma.

"But I know she doesn't do drugs! She wouldn't! And she'd tell me about it too!"

"Did Anna say anything to you about the murders back in August? Any comments about it at all?"

"Just that it was freaking her out, and a great way to start high school. There was something weird though," and she looked thoughtful, and closed her eyes for a second or two.

"We're talking about having to walk by that closet upstairs every day, where they found Aura. And I go: 'It's creepy to walk by there!' And then she goes: 'Yeah, but downstairs where the janitor died is worse. I'm never goin' downstairs there again.' And I go: 'So what difference does it make?' And she goes: 'It just does.' I thought that was kind of weird."

It wasn't weird at all, of course, given Anna's story. Here was a little evidence at least that Anna believed she had seen something "downstairs there." It made me want to believe even more that Anna's story was not some sort of hallucination. We told Abby that we had to get back to the Biology lab. After taking a few steps away I said to Emma:

"That girl's a little traumatized by everything too, I think."

Emma nearly spat out scorn.

"Yeah, right, as if any of you could understand trauma at all."

I stopped and glared at her.

"Your family's not the only one in this! Yes, I do understand trauma! I understand it because when I see Anna dying I want to reach back into the past, shake the universe, and change history! In my imagination she's dying again and again, and I'm watching her, watching her for 3 days straight, wondering what I might have done to stop it, and I'm not sleeping and barely eating because I'm blaming myself for not going to the cops right away - with or without her! Blaming myself for not seeing what might happen to her! And then I try to ignore her memory by running or reading or watching old movies at 3 A.M. or anything to stop thinking about her and about what might happen next! I'd like to remember what a normal stomach feels like! I'd like to remember Anna and smile at my thoughts instead of feeling guilty! I'd like to remember what it feels like to look up into a clear October sky and not add ten thousand black clouds to it! So, yes, I understand trauma to the mind and soul! I've still got it!"

I was maybe too forceful, but for the first time I felt that Emma was not the dominant one in our conversation. She looked apologetic even. After a very long and silent pause, she asked:

"Which movies?"

"What do you mean?" I said this with something of a growl.

"Which movies did you watch at 3 A.M.?"

I didn't say anything at first, so I could calm down.

"One of them was *The Searchers*."

"Sounds appropriate," and she smiled slightly.

"Ever see it?"

"No. Is it a detective movie?"

"Not really. It's a classic Western with John Wayne."

"I don't watch Westerns."

"Why not?"

"They're boring."

"If you've never seen a Western, how do you know they're boring?"

"Okay, okay, they just seem boring."

"Well, if you only see one Western, you should see *The Searchers*. I've heard all the film schools have their students study it. It's about a Confederate veteran who goes looking for his niece. The Indians kidnapped her. It takes him years, and you get the impression when he finds her, he's going to kill her."

"What?! Why would he do that?"

"Because he's a racist. He thinks she's been contaminated after living with the Indians and turned into a squaw."

"So what happens?"

"I won't spoil it for you. You'll have to watch it for yourself."

"Oh, thanks a lot!"

There was another pause.

"So, what other movies did you see?" she asked.

I could tell that Emma was trying to make me feel better, and to apologize, very indirectly, for her "trauma" comment. She's tough, and saying sorry isn't easy for her. Maybe this is the best she can do. I don't hold grudges, so I accepted this cinematic conversation.

"One was a murder mystery, except the audience knows everything, and the mystery is how the villain will get caught. It's called *Dial M for Murder* by Alfred Hitchcock."

"Never saw that one either. What happens in it?"

"There's this husband who hires a hit-man to kill his wife, because she's cheating on him. He's got the perfect crime mapped out to make it look like a robbery plus murder, instead of a hit. But the hit-man bungles it, and the wife ends up being able to kill him during the struggle."

"Cool! So the husband gets caught eventually?"

"You'll have to see it for yourself," I repeated with some spite.

"Okay, okay, I get it."

We had entered the Biology lab, and Emma returned to her curious cat. But as she stood at the table, she showed no interest in cat anatomy at the moment.

"You never answered me," she said suddenly. "Is there anything we can do now about clearing my uncle's name?"

I gave her the bad news about my visit to the police.

"If I could've convinced Anna herself to go, maybe they would've thought more of the story. But now…"

"Now there's nothing."

"Which means," I said slowly, "that we have to make something happen."

"Like what?"

"I have an idea, but you'll be directly involved."

"How?" and Emma frowned.

"I want you to confess to the murders."

October 13

There is usually a problem with brilliant ideas. Other people don't think they're brilliant. The history of science is full of stories like that: Joseph Lister, Louis Pasteur, and the Wright Brothers. The other problem with brilliant ideas is that they take a long time to develop. I'll admit I was not yet sure how I wanted to work this out to force something to happen in the case. Emma wanted to know right then what I was talking about: you can imagine she thought I had lost my mind. In fact she did say I had lost my mind, and put a very nasty adjective in front of the word "mind" to emphasize her opinion. But I had this image in my head, and I thought it might help us.

Emma was a tough-minded girl, and she was strong physically. Those two things don't always have to be together in a person. I've known some weak, skinny kids who could go crazy with stubbornness. But Emma obviously had strength: she didn't go along with the crowd. She ran into them with the SUV of her personality.

What I had in mind yesterday was Emma somehow becoming friendly with Uncle Al. She would become maybe even a little too friendly, and then one day she finds a special moment when she whispers to Uncle Al that she'll tell him a secret. Friends tell each other secret things, even the worst secret things about themselves, so that the friendship deepens. It increases trust. I could see her whispering into Uncle Al's ear and gleefully confessing that she had murdered 3 people. I would be in the area to watch the scene, to see the reaction in Uncle Al's face. Sure: if Uncle Al is guilty, then this would be rather dangerous. That's why the confession would have to happen in public, with enough people around to prevent him from doing anything. But I was also counting on Emma's physical strength to counterbalance any violent reaction from him.

On the other hand if Uncle Al is innocent, which I highly doubt, then her confession would… what? Shock him? Make him think she's nutzoid? Send him to the police? Unless I am missing something, I don't think anything could happen. Emma could always just say she was pranking him to get a reaction. He would think she's just another crazy girl: there are bunches of crazy girls out there. They tend to sit on the left side of the cafeteria. Of course, as I've said, Emma comes across as tough, even though she is somewhat pretty. (No, this is not a clue that I'm a boy. It's a clue that I'm objective and can see all sides.)

But I'm betting that Uncle Al can't be too choosy about his female companionship. I'm betting that if Emma shows any kind of flirting toward Uncle Al, there'll be puddles of drool around his feet. The problem is getting Emma to go along with this brilliant plan: like I said, other people don't always see how brilliant an idea really is. Emma is one of those other people, for now at least.

So I thought I should get somebody to back us up: a professional, in case things got rough. Since the police weren't interested, I'd have to look for a local Sam Spade. Problem: no money for hiring a private detective. Second problem: how to convince a private detective that he – or she – should work for me, a 14-year old kid, even if I did have money, on a case the police claim is solved.

Solution: check the phone book and the Internet. Find some private eyes, like Hall and Oates, and see if they have a website. If they don't, I can offer my website-building knowledge to put them on the W3, in exchange for some back-up. And the odds are that a private detective with a small ad might appreciate this new way of advertising. Another brilliant idea!

So today after school here's what happened. I had a list of 3 agencies pretty close to each other downtown. At the first one I couldn't get past the secretary. But any detective with a secretary was probably too prosperous anyway. At the second office it was obvious the place was out of business. Here my theory seemed to be working: a small ad meant the agency wasn't doing the best. I still had 90 minutes before I had to be home for supper. (My parents believed I was practicing soccer and trying to make the team: except I don't want to be on the team: who wants to play one of the most boring, socialist games on the planet?) But to conserve time and at least kind of look like I had done something physical, I ran halfway to the third office. If this were strike three, I'd have to rethink my brilliant idea, or go to an agency that had a larger ad and run the risk of complete rejection.

But it wasn't strike three. The agency was in an office building almost 100 years old, and most of it seemed pretty empty. I remembered my parents saying that it used to be the main office building for important lawyers and businessmen back in the good old days. But these aren't the good old days. The directory showed a foot doctor and a chiropractor on the ground floor. The whole second floor was vacant. The detective was on the third floor: I used a wide stairway. I didn't trust the elevator. It looked older than my grandmother.

The door had *Frank Stark, Private Investigator* in fading letters. A sign said to press the buzzer. After a pause somebody unlocked the door and coughed. Then the door swung open, but nobody was visible at first. Then a very thin man stepped out from behind the door. He wasn't happy to see me.

"What could you want?"

The question seemed directed at a third person. Mr. Stark could be near 60, or he could be near 45, but look like 60, because of the use of cancer sticks to poison his body. It was hard to say. Maybe I'll ask him his age later.

"The doctors are downstairs," he offered in a hoarse voice, and then he coughed. But as he looked at me he could tell that my feet and spine were in perfect condition. Then he added: "And I'm not buyin' magazines, unless you're sellin' *Grit*."

I thought this might refer to the John Wayne movie *True Grit*, but later an Internet search revealed it to be an ancient "happy news" newspaper, often sold by children in Kansas or North Dakota to earn pocket change. Circulation must be around 317.

"No, I have a case, a criminal case."

"Then go to the cops."

"They say the case is closed. Actually it's not a case: it's 3 murder cases, but they're probably all done by the same person."

Mr. Stark squinted his eyes at me.

"You're talkin' 'bout the deaths at the high school, huh?"

I nodded and waited to be let in, and then I would ask to open a window. He was still studying me.

"You've gone to the cops already, huh?"

"Like I said, they think my story is just kids over-reacting, teenage hysteria." I paused. "I have to admit, they do have a simpler explanation for the deaths than mine. To be fair, it does seem like hysteria and exaggeration."

I introduced myself at this point, and Mr. Stark squinted at me again. He coughed and said: "Look, I can tell you're a real smart kid. What are you, 'bout 14 or so?"

I admitted that year 15 was not too far away.

"I don't handle stuff like this. Way out o' my league." He walked back to the rear of the office, which I interpreted as an invitation to enter. I coughed a few times, and asked if I could open the window.

"Suit yourself, but it's a little chilly today." Then he added: "I'll bet you're one o' those anti-smokin' nuts."

I wanted to praise him as a regular Sherlock Ho-Hum in the deduction department, but decided just to nod and smile. Why insult somebody I was trying to convince to help with the case?

The office showed certificates from the police department: so Mr. Stark had been a policeman. A few trophies for bowling, and various cameras with huge telephoto lenses, sat on badly painted shelves. There were also large parabolic microphones, recorders, piles of tapes, both audio and video, and a stuffed raccoon. The raccoon seemed to be smiling at me.

"People usually ask about the raccoon," he said.

"Yes, was he a pet?"

"He was my first case." He fooled around with a large cigar, and so I coughed slightly again, and he remembered that I was an "anti-smokin' nut." He dropped the cigar on his desk and said: "Had an old woman who was sure somebody was breakin' into her house all the time and stealin' her stuff up in the attic. The cops got tired o' answerin' her calls o' course. They just thought she was nuts. So she ends up callin' me, so since she was able to pay pretty good, I just said I'd spend the night up in the attic and catch the guy." He picked up the cigar and pointed at the raccoon. "There's the guy!" Then he put the cigar in the corner of his mouth and said: "Speakin' o' bein' able to pay pretty good, that's gonna be a problem with you, ain't it?"

Again I had to admit he was right: my piggy bank was on a diet.

"Well, it don't really matter. Look, you're a nice kid 'n' all that, but there's another problem. You're under 18. I can't take no money from ya anyway. Ain't ethical 'n' prob'ly ain't legal, 'n' that's a fact, since I'd need ya to sign a contract for my services."

I hadn't counted on that: but who would think to make a law like that anyway? I really hate it when the government becomes a baby-sitter and spoils everything. So I asked him just to hear my version of the 3 deaths, complete with Uncle Al coming out as the main suspect at the end. I was encouraged when, after a few minutes, he grabbed a yellow legal pad and started writing.

"Here's the deal I was thinking of," I said. "I noticed you don't have a website." In fact I also noticed only an electric typewriter on a metal stand: he didn't have a computer at all. "That's the newest thing businesses need to go into the

21st century. I know how to make one for you, and get you on a really cheap server. In exchange, maybe you could help me to investigate this janitor."

"That still means I'm workin' for ya, kid, and I told ya it ain't legal."

I pointed to the equipment on the shelves and said: "Well, maybe in exchange for website work you'd let me use some of that stuff."

Mr. Stark laughed and then started choking. He walked quickly over to the window, cleared his throat with the sound of a shovel skidding across gravel, and then spat out the window.

"Look out below!" he mumbled. I hid my disgust.

"You're not as smart as I thought, if you think I'm gonna let you have any o' my 'quipment," he grunted.

"You can check my record at school. I'm an honor student and I've never received a demerit or even a detention. How about if I come here after school and just clean up or answer the phone? I'll do it for free. You can consider me your apprentice. You would be the master, the master detective!"

Okay, this was just slightly dramatic, and he knew it.

"Apprentices need real masters. Look, I told ya, I don't do criminal cases. Mainly I do…motel work. You know, divorce cases. I follow people around 'n' photograph their cars 'n' license plates when they're someplace they shouldn't be."

I was almost out of bullets. So I aimed and took a last shot:

"So now you've got a chance to do something important, maybe catch a serial killer, instead of breaking up marriages."

"I don't break up marriages! They're already broken by the time I get involved."

So it happened anyway: I ended up insulting him. My smart-aleck mouth had ruined any chance I might've had. Sometimes my talent with words gets too powerful. So I started walking to the door and said:

"Thanks for listening. Sorry if I insulted what you do on your job."

"It's just the reality of your situation, kid. You've got to know your limitations!"

I stopped and said: "I'm 14 years old: I don't have any limitations!"

He didn't say any more until I touched the doorknob.

"Maybe… I can give you pointers, that's all. I really can't get involved."

So I thought: you don't always get what you want, but if you try sometimes, you get what you need.

Maybe "pointers" were all I would need.

October 14

On Saturday everything fell apart. Well, maybe not everything, but it felt like everything fell apart! (And be careful, guys: if you're trying to guess when I'm really writing this, remember that I play with dates, and sometimes with figs and raisins. Today doesn't have to be Saturday, October 14th: it could be any day after a Saturday!)

It started with the mail. A letter came for me: no return address, and I was positive the handwriting on the envelope was identical to the one Sam showed me, the one he thought was from Anna. I opened it with a sharp knife, and pulled out the paper. It was a typical, unlined piece of white computer paper with perforations at the top and bottom. A dot-matrix printer was used: I was positive again that the same person was behind this letter and the one Sam received. My envelope, however, did have a stamp and it was canceled: somebody had sent it yesterday.

"Get off the case!"

"Get off the case!"

"Get off the case!"

This is what the letter said: all the way down, probably 40 times or so. It was unsettling at first, to say the least! But then I started laughing: this was so hokey! Somebody besides me had been watching too many old movies. I walked around my room and looked at it, while Bach's *Well-Tempered Clavier* was playing. "Get off the case!" Who knew that I was involved in a "case" anyway? Anna had known, but she was dead. Frank Stark, the detective, knew about it now, but it was impossible that he sent this. How could he have sent the other letter to Sam's house? So that made no sense.

Emma knew: but she wants the case solved, so her uncle's name will be cleared. I'm the only one doing any kind of digging for her: why would she send me an anonymous letter telling me to get off the case? Emma's not that kind of girl: she would just tell me directly, maybe too directly, that my help was no longer needed.

My cousin Martika and her boyfriend, Steve Cadosia, knew about the case. They met Anna, and saw Sam at her funeral, and Martika kind of guessed he might've been the second witness. But they did not know that before the funeral, and Sam's first threatening letter was already at his house. And yet: let's assume that somehow they knew about Sam. Martika is another Emma: a secret letter just doesn't fit her combat-ready personality. Steve? He didn't seem the type either: doing something like this, especially without Martika's consent, didn't fit him. So I thought it was impossible that they could have sent Sam that letter.

Lana? She heard me accuse Uncle Al of being a sleazeball, and of maybe murdering Anna. But she didn't know Sam was involved in (maybe) hearing the murder of Mr. Laurenz. Conclusion: also impossible.

An outsider? Perhaps somebody knew about me and about the case. Perhaps they had overheard me talking to Emma, or Sam, or even Anna, and now they were trying to scare me with this old-school threat. I thought I had been careful at school, and that nobody had been in the area, whenever I was talking to anyone. But who knows? Conclusion: not impossible.

Finally I suppose there's Uncle Al: he would want me "off the case" for sure! But how would he know anything about me? He had some contact with Sam through the Work Crew. But he can't possibly know that I think he's a suspect! And if Uncle Al's really a serial killer, I wouldn't be reading a dumb letter like this straight out of a bad movie.

I'd be dead.

The doorbell rang. My long lost cousin Martika came to visit me.

"What've you been doing?" she asked. I pointed to the stereo and said:

"Listening to Bach's *Well-Tempered Clavier* and increasing my intelligence. What about you?"

"You are so out of it, it's not even funny." I turned the volume down and smiled:

"You should try it: Bach can definitely replace all those brain cells you lost with M. C. Hammer and Milli Vanilli."

"Very funny as always. Listen: I heard something yesterday, something you won't believe."

I said nothing. After a long pause she asked:

"Well?"

"You're right: I don't believe it."

Martika expanded her vocabulary of foolgarisms on me. Then she said:

"Are you gonna listen or not? This is important!"

"Let's hear it, and then I'll tell you if it's important or not."

"I heard some kid say Anna was murdered!" and Martika acted like she had just revealed the deepest secret in the universe.

"Who said this? Was it a girl?"

"Good guess!"

"A girl with short reddish blond hair and strange gray eyes?"

Martika was impressed, and I have to admit I was just a little proud of myself.

"Yeah. How do you know?"

"Her name's Abby, and she was Anna's best friend. Or claims she was at least. I broke up a fight she was in a few days ago, and she told me she doesn't believe the drug story behind Anna's death. So now she's coming out and saying Anna was murdered?"

"Yeah, she was going off on somebody in the hall and yelled it: 'Anna was murdered! Somebody murdered her!' I guess the kid she was talking to didn't believe it."

"Any idea who she was talking to?"

"Some girl. Little freshman."

"Blond, skinny, doesn't sound very intelligent, and a clone of 30 million other blond skinny 14-year old girls?"

"Sounds right."

No doubt it was Amber, she of the long sing-song vowels. Abby seemed to have high-strung fits when Amber was around. Amber needed to concentrate on consonants: maybe Abby's reaction would be less hysterical.

"This isn't important."

"What? She comes right out and says Anna was murdered and that's not important? Maybe she knows something or saw something."

"She doesn't know anything. She's wishing and hoping and praying that Anna didn't commit suicide."

"So, what's next?"

"We wait."

"For what?"

"For another murder. A murder where we can get some evidence, guaranteed."

"How can we do that?"

"By offering him a victim to kill."

Martika was really speechless. She looked at me as if I were an alien from Planet Megatron.

"You've gone nuts. Really, 100% nuts!"

I crossed my eyes and stuck out my tongue: Martika was unimpressed by this massive display of talent.

"I'm insane? I'd say the serial killer is the one with mental problems," and I decided to outline the plan taking root in my mind.

"I have a suspect, but I need to tempt him to kill again, so that this time I'd have some evidence. A picture or a videotape, anything."

"And so how do you plan on 'tempting' him this time?"

"The same way he's been tempted so far: with a pretty girl."

"You don't mean me?!"

Well, speaking of temptation, I was tempted to blurt out "I said a pretty girl," but that would have been cruel and insulting, although true. It might also have been painful… for me. Emma was not Barbie material, and Martika was even less so. I was assuming that Emma had more to interest Uncle Al than Martika. And Emma had a direct role in the case through Mr. Laurenz. Anyway, this time I controlled my mouth. But I did have a flash of inspiration.

"You'll be involved. And with Steve, if he wants to."

"What's that mean?"

"To prevent a real murder from happening, we'll have to be in the area when our victim and suspect are together. If the suspect really is a serial killer, then…well, I'm asking you to do something pretty dangerous. But I'm hoping with your Junior ROTC training, and with Steve's as well, that together we could handle him."

"If we need to, I can get some handguns," she said with determination.

"No, absolutely not!"

"Guns are the great equalizers, when you're in something like this." Martika sounded like an expert suddenly.

"They can cause us all kinds of problems too! It's… premature anyway. This plan will take a few weeks. Maybe longer."

"So what is this plan?"

Without mentioning Emma or the janitor by name (I still want to keep things as separate as possible, although it doesn't seem to be working right now! Pretty soon everyone involved will know each other, it seems.) I told her that the plan was for Emma to show Uncle Al some attention, and when they get a little friendlier, and just a little cozy, she will confess to the murders.

"That doesn't make any sense."

"Why? We'll know by his reaction if he's the real killer."

"No you won't: you'll know it only if he's innocent, 'cause if he's the real killer, he'll just be crazy happy to find someone to confess to his crimes!"

Whoops! Sometimes the problem with brilliant ideas is that they aren't so brilliant after all. I was embarrassed and crushed. Her objection was so obvious!

"You're right. You're absolutely right. Why didn't I see that?"

Martika didn't say anything while I shook my head in disgust at my mistake. Then she said: "C'mon cuz, snap out of it. What's Plan B?"

There wasn't a Plan B, because I was positive Plan A was so…brilliant. I sighed: even a genius can have an off day. (Except I really don't know if I'm a genius: never took a test.) I thought quickly.

"We can stick to most of the original idea," I said, trying to salvage what was left. "Maybe she can talk to him about the murders, and wonder how they happened and stuff like that, and then we can see how he reacts. But that might take even longer. I guess I was hoping to solve everything quickly by having her confess. This would be a weaker method, but he still could say or do something that would give us some evidence."

Martika agreed to help in this, and I tried to act confident again. She left for swimming practice. I chased away the embarrassment of Martika finding the hole in Plan A so easily. Something else came to mind: I had a big worry that Uncle Al might not be in the mood any more. Serial killers can go for months and even years between their crimes. It could happen that he's quite satisfied with 3 murders, and won't take any bait thrown at him. That's why I was hoping to provoke him quickly with the phony confession from Emma. I was hoping he would get sloppy and nervous and make a mistake. Then we would have him!

If he is the serial killer. If all of this isn't a fantasy from Anna. I do wonder if I'm not just some silly kid with too much time, too much boredom, too much arrogance, and too much imagination. I keep thinking of that old rule: simple solutions are the best. And really, so far, the police seem to have everything right.

But then I see Anna's face! That face, when she told me how she glimpsed the hanging body and that figure in a uniform! Her face, when she remembered that voice of the man whispering that threat into her ear! Whoever you are in the future and reading this, I wish I could show you Anna's face then, which is now embalmed, bloodless, and waiting for Jesus.

You'd be searching for a killer too!

And anyway, working on the case does beat boredom. So does dodging cars in the school parking lot. On Friday things became very complicated: I was walking down a lane in the parking lot to take a short cut home. I could hear a car coming so I moved over, but the driver - "moron" is the better word - was intentionally steering toward me. I hopped in between two cars, so that he couldn't do anything to me. I knew he wouldn't really hit me, and for a moment I thought about just standing still and daring the idiot to hit me. But I didn't want to take the chance that he would miscalculate. "Narc!" was yelled as the car zipped by, along with the expected obscenities. I memorized the license plate and the kind of car and wrote them down quickly in a notebook.

Thinking lightning wouldn't strike twice, I started off again. But the moron car had circled around and was coming back for a second attack! Again I ran in between some parked cars, but this time I headed for the football field, where there would be too many witnesses, if the punks in the car decided to get out and start something. Again obscenities and the word "Narc" were shouted.

After waiting for a while, I gave up on the idea of walking home and quickly headed for the bus stop. So my narc-reputation was still floating around. It looked like I couldn't count on the short attention span of the druggies to forget me. Maybe they just needed a little more marijuana to erase me out of their minds. Drugs could be my friend after all!

Anyway, back to today and that letter. I picked it up and looked at it again, went over to the stereo, and put on Pat Benatar's Greatest Hits. That's right: *Invincible*, with one of the funkiest guitar parts ever written. After yesterday's adventure I felt sort of invincible. Then I looked at the mysterious "Get off the case!" letter again.

There was only one solution to this mini-mystery, and it made me angry.

I rode my bicycle over to Sam's house. His little brother Josh answered the door.

"I remember you!" he said.

"Good! Is Sam around?"

"No, he's out somewhere. At the store I think." Actually I was happy to hear that.

"Your dad home?"

"No, he's on the road again," and Josh sighed a little. And I was happy to hear that too. Then he asked: "You wanna come in?"

"I think you're probably not supposed to let anybody in unless Sam or your Dad are around."

"It's okay. I like you! You're funny!" and he opened the door more widely and let me in.

"Do you stay at home by yourself a lot?"

"I dunno. Ya wanna watch cartoons?"

I agreed to watch only great cartoons with Bugs Bunny or Daffy Duck. This was not possible, unfortunately, and Josh tuned in something very unfunny. After several minutes I stood up and said I wanted to use the bathroom. Josh pointed down the hallway.

What I wanted to do was find something in Sam's bedroom. As I peeked into the bedroom, I didn't see what I was looking for at first, because of the piles of junk. So I decided to go in and quickly move some things around. A hard plastic cast for a broken arm lay next to a desk. A yellowing 1980's computer sat on a desk, but the machine was partially hidden by a stack of underwear. I moved a mountain of towels next to that, and found what I really didn't want to find.

I went back to Josh and watched the dreadful cartoon with him: the characters were jerking around because of cheap, incompetent animation done in a foreign country. But their motions matched the angry twitching in my body.

"Do you have a computer?" I asked Josh.

"Yeah! Y' wanna see it?"

"Sure. You have any computer games?"

"Only a couple: they're old 'cause the computer's old."

I followed him back to the bedroom, where he uncovered the computer and…a dot-matrix printer.

"Does Sam use this much?"

"I dunno," said Josh with a shrug, "sometimes, I guess, for school and stuff."

"Before you start a game, could I print a page? A little joke for your brother."

I'm sure you know what I typed. When the printer stopped burping, I pulled out the "Get off the case!" letter and compared it to the new one in my hand.

They were identical, complete with the same degree of lightness because the cartridge was worn out. I was furious, seething, but was able to hide it from Josh, who was now playing a primitive computer game of some sort with rabbits. Out of politeness I watched him for a few minutes, then I went back to the living room and paced around, then went back to Josh.

I frowned at the plastic cast and asked Josh about it. He explained that Sam had broken his arm while training for JROTC. This was news! Sam never mentioned that before. Josh said that Sam decided to drop out: he wanted the money from working after school. Besides, the broken arm had happened after only a day or two, and seemed to show bad luck for the future. Sam then pulled up in an old car. He had four plastic bags full of groceries in his hands. I opened the door, and he seemed very surprised.

"Josh let you in? He really shouldn't've done that."

I smiled a little and said: "I know. I already mentioned that to him."

Sam went into the kitchen with the groceries and said: "So, what's up?"

"Another mysterious letter," I said, and pulled out the envelope. "This time it came to me, instead of you."

"Wow! What's going on now?" and he acted stunned.

"I had no idea at first, but then I figured it out."

"Well, you're pretty smart. Even if you are just a freshman," and he smiled a little at this comment. Then his eyes became big as he scanned the letter.

"Yes, I'm pretty smart," and I produced the second page.

"What's that?"

"It's this letter again," I said with my teeth clenched. "Printed by the same dot-matrix printer, with the same cartridge, on the same kind of old paper, as the first one!" and I threw both of the letters onto the kitchen table.

"What were you doing in my room?" and he acted angry.

"Wrong question, and misses the point entirely!"

"I didn't send that to you! Why would I do that?"

"Because I was right the first time, weeks ago! You were never downstairs at the janitor's office when Mr. Laurenz was dying! You never heard anything! You're a fake, a pathetic fake who wants attention! This letter's phony, the other one was phony, those other threats that I thought were from the deadheads were phony: you made them all and sent them to yourself!"

Sam's lower lip trembled. I wondered suddenly if I had been too quick to assume that he was the author. It was always possible that somebody with the exact same kind of dot-matrix printer was behind the letters, and that Sam was the victim of an almost impossible coincidence.

"Sorry."

His one word said I was right, but I might have preferred being wrong again today.

"What's going on?" asked Josh, who looked confused in the doorway.

"Nothing," I said, "your brother just needed a reality check. One that doesn't bounce."

Sam sent Josh back to the computer game. He continued putting groceries away and didn't look at me.

"I don't know if you've noticed, but, you're the only one who hangs around with me."

Actually, no I hadn't noticed: I just assumed that Sam had his older circle of friends from the junior class. And this case prevents me from thinking of anybody much as a friend. I guess I always looked at Sam and Anna as people who fit into the explanation of a possible killing spree. I know I was beginning to consider Anna a friend, and that's why her death was not something I could get over quickly. With Sam being older, I never thought that he could think of me as a friend.

So I was wrong about something after all!

And don't worry: no, I'm not telling you yet if I'm a boy or a girl! That has nothing to do here anyway with basic trust and fungifying the case!

"I just thought…I thought the only way to…you know, keep talking to you was to keep the case going, to give you something to keep going after. Because…because nothing new was happening about it." He looked humiliated. "It was kind of nice to have somebody call me, or wait for me to show up at school."

Sam Worcester, The Lonely Guy, so lonely he would want a new freshman with no obvious social skills for his friend to "hang around" with now and then.

"Did you lie to me about hearing the noises when Mr. Laurenz was killed?"

"No, no! That's still true. That happened."

"I think I'll be the one to decide if it's still true or not."

I left and went back home, still angry at times, and then just thinking about what to do next. I sighed and thought: it's time to get Plan B rolling. Emma needs to tell me for sure that she will act as bait for Uncle Al.

Except I was hit by a distant memory: weeks ago Emma had said she would gladly kill the person responsible for murdering her uncle. I didn't believe her then. I thought it was just a typical exaggeration. But now, with my lapse today about Plan A, I was wondering if I would be making a mistake by having Emma be the bait. This was depressing: and that's why I was thinking that everything was falling apart. And if I get anybody else involved in this, I'd be breaking my own rule about trying to limit the number of people who knew my theory of the crime.

I've already told you that I don't trust people who lack confidence. I especially can't trust my own judgment if I lack confidence: so I have to stop this self-doubt and stop it fast. Emma thought the plan "sucked" from the start, and didn't want to be part of it. So if I shouldn't use Emma or Martika, then I would have to break my rule. It was that simple. But who should be the bait?

And right now, as I'm writing this, I'm having a new brilliant idea. My usual self-confidence is back! Maybe everything isn't falling apart, just coming together in a new way. It's obvious who the bait for Plan B should be. I need someone who is on the edge about the deaths here at school, who looks pretty, but isn't going to be thinking too much.

I need a Twixie.

October 16

So today it was time for a Return to the Valley of the Twixies. The Twixies' area of the cafeteria tended to float, but right now it was near the emergency exit. Squeals of the worst teenager clichés, squeals of pain, squeals of delight, and squeals of hysteria echoed from this area. The Twixies themselves were usually divided by class, but sometimes you might see freshmen mingling with sophomores, or juniors with seniors. This cross-pollination could mean even louder cries of OMIGOD or R-U-SERIOUS or GETOUT. After you got used to it, you could ignore it. But there were times when the squealing was so loud, most everyone stopped what they were doing and looked at the Valley of the Twixies. Worst of all, you could never tell when one or more of the Twixies would break out and leave the valley to infect a different part of the cafeteria. Usually this happened when a Twixie had found true love, which really meant of course that they had chosen some Poor Unsuspecting Guy to obsess about. If the PUG responded in any way, he was doomed, at least temporarily. And if the PUG responded too deeply by going all funky submarine on the Twixie, his soul was doomed forever.

It was time for Sam – he owed me now - to become a PUG and bag a Twixie for Plan B. And how do I know that a Twixie will help in this?

Because, you see, Twixie is school slang for a Totally Whacked-out Chick. (Nobody knew who coined this word, but I'll admit it might have been me.) And since this plan was close to being totally whacked out as well, it just seemed logical to use a Twixie to entice Uncle Al.

I spotted Sam in the cafeteria and waved to him. He seemed surprised and relieved, and even smiled a little bit.

"I didn't think you'd want to talk to me about anything again."

"Well, you're going to pay a price for wasting my time on your phony letters."

He turned red and didn't say anything. I explained Plan B to him: he was going to talk a good-looking Twixie, preferably a junior or senior, into helping us put Uncle Al off his guard.

"How am I supposed to do that?"

"How many Twixies over there do you know?"

"A couple, I guess. Just from my classes."

"Today, right now, you're going to go over there and start a conversation with the most likely candidate for our plan."

"That's nuts! I can't do that."

"What's nuts is sending me and yourself phony threats to get attention." I looked as grim as I could. "You're in this now, up to your neck! Don't tell me what you can't do! Now get over there and pick out the best Twixie for this! Specifically one who knew Aura Malper."

My parents say I have a dominating personality. Maybe that's why I don't have any friends in my definition of the word.

Sam looked like he was about to be executed. I have to admit: as he walked away, I wondered if I was doing this partly to humiliate him in revenge for his stupid fake threats. It didn't matter: I had concluded that we had to offer Uncle Al new, fresh, female bait, and that's what we would be doing.

And as back-up to Plan B, Plan C went into operation. I was in charge of that. Plan C was identical to Plan B, except that the bait was a freshman girl, somebody I knew would help, somebody who was pretty, somebody who wasn't afraid of a fight.

Anna's self-proclaimed best friend, Abby.

So I looked around and found her with a flock of seagulls who would probably end up in the Valley of the Twixies soon. I walked over to Abby and asked to talk with her about something. No, I will not tell you the reaction of the seagulls, since that would give away my gender. If they became wide-eyed and started whispering and giggling when Abby got up, then you would know that I have to be a boy. If they had no reaction, then you would know that I'm a girl.

You can go outside during lunch to a large patio. Since it was pretty cool today, not too many kids were there. So I motioned we should go there to talk.

"I've decided to tell you a secret about Anna's death."

"Omigod! OMIGOD! I'm freaking out already!"

I was right. Abby was a Twixie: she just didn't know it yet.

"Look at me! You'll fungify everything, and I mean everything, if you can't control yourself! Now I'm going to tell you something, and I don't want you to say a word after you hear it."

I'm not a physical person, but I grabbed her arm and whispered: "It's likely that Anna was murdered."

Abby's mouth opened, but I squeezed her arm as hard as I could and said: "Not one word!"

"Okay, okay, omigod, I knew it! I just knew it!"

As I unrolled the role Anna may have played as witness to the hanging of Mr. Laurenz, Abby kept shaking her head, and then almost started crying.

"Why didn't she tell me about this? I'm her best friend!"

"We've gone through this. I don't know. All I know is that she asked me to do something about the murder."

"But that's what I don't get! Why you? Why didn't she ask me?"

"Again, all I can tell you is that she asked me to do something."

I decided not to tell her that Anna came to me because she thought I was smart, and that Anna did not go to her because she's a hyper Twixie-in-training who would just panic.

"Look at me: do you want to help us find her killer?"

"Well, duuuh! And who's 'us'?"

"You're not the only who wants the truth. That's assuming that we aren't wrong."

"I thought you said you know she was murdered!"

"No, I said 'probably' murdered. There's always the possibility that all of this is wrong. But with your help, we can verify our suspicions."

"Okay, so what do I have to do to help?"

"Do you know the janitor named Al?"

"OMIGOD! Did he kill Anna?"

"Will you stop that?"

"Okay, okay. But is he the killer?"

"No, he's the suspect. This is America. Innocent until proven guilty, remember?"

"Okay, okay, but, so, what, I mean, how do I help?"

The prospect of becoming involved in this was obviously rattling her.

"The plan is for you to get Uncle Al… interested… in you."

"What's 'interested' sposta mean?"

"You know exactly what it means. Can you do that or not?"

"Oh, wow, I don't know," and she looked confused.

"Do you want to help solve Anna's death, and maybe Aura's and Mr. Laurenz's as well?

"Well, yeah, duuh, sure! But, wow, that sounds, I don't know, risky, you know?"

"Of course I know. That's why there will always be some of us around, in case things get out of control."

"You think the guy's a pervert, and that's why he killed Anna?"

"No, I think he's a pervert and that's why he killed Aura Malper. Mr. Laurenz and Anna were collateral damage."

"What's that mean?"

"It's a military term. It means they got in the way unexpectedly. They saw too much maybe. And so… they had to die."

"Wow, I can't believe you know all this."

"I don't know it. It's all based on Anna's story, and I'm not sure it's true."

"But it makes sense! It makes sense! That's why she died!"

"No, it also makes sense that she could've died because of drugs. Even if you don't want to believe it."

"So, how do I get him 'interested' in me?"

I told her she would find out by the end of the day. First, I needed to see how Sam was doing with Plan B. And I couldn't believe my luck! He was talking to one of the work crew, one of the Lana Lights! She had to be a junior or senior, since she buzzed around Lana. On top of that she was good-looking, in a way. Good enough for Uncle Al, I thought. Of course, just talking to her didn't mean anything yet.

As I was soon to find out.

Sam brought her over to me.

"This is Allie. She was a friend of Aura's," he said. Allie was a typical Twixie in looks: blond, designer jeans that were too tight, and the ancient trick of a double wad of tissues in her milk compartment. But she almost sneered at me and frowned the big ugly. Her skepticism was not well hidden.

"But, you must be just a freshman!" she said, as if Sam had told her to shake hands with Moses or Buddha or Jesus, and it turned out to be a runny-nosed kindergartner.

"And you must be just another friend of Aura's," I said with the same amount of skepticism. Actually, I almost used the phrase "dumb, 62 I.Q. Twixie" to her, instead of "friend of Aura's." But my people skills are improving.

"So what do you know about Aura?" she asked.

"How much did Sam tell you?"

"Like, that you guys know something the police don't know about Aura's murder."

"They know it. They just don't believe it." I paused. "How do I know I can trust you to keep your mouth shut?" I asked that a little too impolitely, but I thought I had to sound pretty tough right now.

Foul fowl-rhyming curses rained down on me from her mouth. Allie looked hurt and stupid all at the same time, which softened my approach.

"Sorry, but we're about to do something dangerous," I said. "Allie, look at me."

She cursed me again and, as she looked at me, asked why she needed to look at me. No, I was not trying to hypnotize her!

"Because if our theory's right, someone could get seriously hurt, so we need people we can trust to stay quiet."

I have rather large grayish eyes: I haven't told you that yet. Allie was weakening and seemed to be debating more deeply whether she wanted to join us in our possibly foolish crusade for justice. She whispered to Sam: why was he involved in this?

"Because I heard something when Mr. Laurenz was dying, and it made me think it wasn't suicide."

"You're on the work-crew with Lana?" I asked, knowing the answer. She did not recognize me from our two previous encounters when I spoke with Lana: the day before Anna died, and the day of Anna's funeral. She nodded.

"What do you think of Uncle Al, the janitor?" I said slowly and grimly.

Allie was slow, but she could understand the implication.

"Get out!"

I nodded.

"Omigod! OMIGOD!"

"Mouth…shut!" I warned.

"But shouldn't the guys on the work crew know?! Omigod!"

"Nobody can know! You can't tell anyone, not Lana, nobody knows!"

And speaking of Lana, you might wonder why I didn't get her for this job. She was in the upper grades, pretty, not too bright, everything I said I was looking for. But something about Lana made me unsure of her. Her back-and-forths between occasional intelligence and usual dumb-blond stereotypes kept me from asking her about joining us. Besides, if she did think that Uncle Al was a "cool guy" and "a nice guy" like she said, then she would be the last one to believe us, and the first one to alert him.

Lana was like Arithmetic tests from the special kids: she didn't add up.

So Allie seemed nicely shocked now: the hard part was coming next.

"That explains why he acted kind of weird maybe! That one time, yeah, omigod!" and she was obviously remembering something.

"Talk to us."

"Okay, okay, it was kind of freaky, now that I think about it, y' know? It was the afternoon before they found Anna upstairs." Allie closed her eyes. When she opened them again, they were extremely wide, as if she were actually seeing everything again from the day of the murder. "Al told us not to bother going upstairs that day. Like, he said, like, he already checked everything and it wasn't that dirty. He already took care of it. Like, that had never happened before. And then he goes: 'Just do the girls' restroom in the basement.' And we go, like, 'Great!' 'Cause then we get out early, y' know? And then he followed us and talked and talked about stuff."

"What kind of stuff?" I asked.

"You know, like, movies he saw then, and bands and stuff. He's pretty cool about stuff like that, y' know? But, now, now I wonder! Like, leaving early, that never happened before! It just seemed really great to get out early, y' know?"

"So, which movies? And which bands did he talk about?"

"Stuff on cable he saw, I don't know, like, I wasn't paying real close attention, y' know? He was kind of boring us about this one. Maybe it was an old war movie, or science fiction or something."

"Yeah, he talks sometimes about movies to me too," said Sam. "Not much though."

" 'Not much'? He's always talking about something to us!"

"And it's obvious why," I commented. Except it wasn't obvious to Allie.

"Like, why's it so obvious?"

"Because you're girls, and Sam isn't. But this movie: you don't remember anything about the title?"

"Oh I don't know! Why's it such a big deal?"

"It could be a clue of some sort. So think!"

During the pause I have to admit I was rather excited about Allie's story. Keeping the girl work crew away from the very restroom where Anna was later found dead: was that just a coincidence? Was Anna already in there, dying from drugs forced down her throat? Or was Uncle Al just getting everything ready by that time?

Or was it just a coincidence?

"Maybe it was called *Forgotten Planet* or something."

"Do you mean *Forbidden Planet* perhaps?"

"Yeah, that sounds right. What could that mean?"

I said nothing to them at the moment. Again, it could mean absolutely nothing. But it was an interesting choice for Uncle Al to be blabbering about. *Forbidden Planet* was one of the best science-fiction movies from the 1950's, mainly because it's based on a Shakespeare play called *The Tempest*. The movie concerns a squadron of astronauts sent to investigate crimes on a planet that's being colonized. Or was, because every one of the colonists has been murdered in their first years on the planet, except for a scientist and his daughter. It seems an invisible monster attacked everyone and tore their bodies apart: and when only the scientist and his daughter were left, the attacks stopped. The scientist is something of an archeologist, and he knows that a superior race called the Krell once lived on the planet. But they were also killed off by the invisible monster, and their advanced technology could not save them.

I won't spoil the ending for you. But this was a very interesting choice for Uncle Al to be talking about on the day of Anna's death: a movie about an invisible, mass-murdering monster.

"So is it a clue?" asked Sam. I shrugged and looked at Allie.

"Here's the plan: we want you to become 'friendlier' with Al."

"You mean, like, I'd want him? Like, a boyfriend? No way!"

"Look, we have no courtroom evidence, because Anna's dead, but everything she told us seems to check out. If he stalked and killed her, he cleaned up the only loose end. We need to get something new on him."

"What about Sam?"

"I'll repeat: we have no courtroom evidence. That's why we have to trap him somehow. If you were ever alone with him, we'd be nearby, so that nothing happens. But first, you've got to make him notice you, and I mean sexually."

"You want me to make him stalk me?!"

"That sums it up."

Again a foul curse was heard. This was not looking very hopeful.

"I think it'll work," said Sam quietly. "You're just as pretty as Aura, even more. We'll be sure he can't do anything."

"How?"

"I'll get you a small walkie-talkie for your purse," I said. "Whenever you're with him, just turn it on so we can hear everything."

Allie looked at Sam and then at me. Finally she agreed, although it was a glum decision. I told her to begin this afternoon: start conversations with him, smile more, maybe even touch him on the arm and laugh at appropriate moments. I suggested she tell him she really likes his new look, if she can say it with a straight face.

"Can you do this or not?" I asked Allie. "It would help us to find out finally if he's really the killer."

"He's gonna think I'm weird or something."

"Only if you come on too strong to him. That's a mistake: you want him to come after you." Then I added: "I think Aura and Anna and Mr. Laurenz deserve this."

So she said yes. That meant I could put Plan C with Abby on hold. I was afraid too many girls falling all over Uncle Al suddenly would cause him to get suspicious. So I would have to tell her to wait.

Now I turned to Sam.

"You drove today, I hope?"

"Yeah, why?"

"Because later it'll be time for Plan D."

October 18

I had to do homework, and got tired of writing. Some very interesting things have happened since then. First, you're probably wondering what Plan D was, or is. Very simple: follow Uncle Al wherever he goes after school.

Very simple became very interesting. So we sit in the parking lot and wait for him to leave around 5:00. Out he comes 10 minutes early. So we follow Uncle Al for a few blocks, when he stops to visit a watering hole. Sam wanted to stay in the car and wait, but I thought that would be a waste. This was a great time to take a look inside that van.

"What if it's got an alarm?" asked Sam.

"Look at that piece of scrap metal!" I said. "It doesn't have an alarm! But if it does, get ready to roll!"

So I got out and nonchalantly began walking around the van. The driver's door was locked. So were the passenger's and the side doors, but the rear door! It had a looseness to it: not quite open, but not quite tight. With just a little help it opened, and I was able to examine the area quickly. Beer cans, toolkits, beer cans, auto parts, beer cans, empty snack bags, and beer cans formed a carpet: I was expecting an orange shag rug, but Uncle Al treated his van like your basic pig-sty.

Sam appeared and was wide-eyed.

"How'd you get it open?"

"Luck and effort. Get back to the car and if he comes out here, honk the horn."

"Is there anything that…?"

"I don't know yet, now get back."

I moved around the "carpet" a little and looked for any kind of possible evidence. Behind a seat was a wooden box with a padlock on it. That of course seemed really interesting. But it might just be drill bits, or jigsaw blades, or a baseball card collection. I was tempted to take it: I had already just committed my first official crime by breaking into the van. Why not go all the way and steal the box? Such is the slippery slope of sin! After you commit one crime, the next one gets easier. And then after a while you stop noticing that what you're doing is wrong. That's how you explain people who work at death camps for the Stalins and Hitlers of the world. On the other hand my intentions are to stop a crime, to catch a murderer. Wouldn't that justify a very minor theft?

No, because even if the box were full of human heads Uncle Al would walk out of any court a free man. I knew enough about the rules here: evidence obtained illegally is not evidence. Dirty Harry 101. So, since I couldn't open up the mystery box, I looked in some of the toolboxes, just to be sure. Nothing in the first, and nothing in the second, until I pulled out the tray on the top.

Arctic cold ran from my neck to my feet, and I shivered. I almost felt my mind leaving my body and watching myself staring at an impossible sight in the toolbox. Worse, they were staring back at me! No, these did not belong in a toolbox! I picked one up and touched its face. These would be hard to explain. They weren't direct evidence of murder, but they might help. I put the tray back, hopped out, and shut the door.

"Let's get out of here," I told Sam as I got into his car.

"Don't you want to follow him any more?"

"No."

"What's wrong? What did you see?"

"Nothing. Take me downtown, please. I need to take care of something. I'll take a bus home."

Sam was extremely nervous now. You would think I would be the nervous one, after committing my first crime. But there was a quiver in his voice when he asked:

"You saw something in there. What was it?"

"Nothing, I told you that."

"I don't believe that."

"Good: sounds like we're even."

Sam knew what I meant, and didn't say anything until I left. Okay, so I was still punishing him for his little tricks to get attention. So what? It's my case!

I was hoping that Frank Stark would still be in his office. Not everyone takes off at 5:00 for home. Of course if he had a client, he might be out following somebody himself. But I was lucky today: business was bad.

"You again?" he said. Mr. Stark immediately turned around and walked back to his desk. At least he didn't shut the door in my face.

"Still playing detective at your school?" he grunted.

"Things became more serious recently. I need a favor, a small one," and I pulled out the license plate number of the car that I played chicken with. The paper also had the van's number. "Can you find out who owns these cars?"

Mr. Stark looked at the numbers and said: "I still got some friends in the department who can look things up for me. This part o' your 'murder' case?" and he used an ironic tone for pronouncing the word "murder."

"Sort of, it seems there's more than one case now. The new one deals with attempted murder and drug-dealing."

"Really? Nothin' on the news about that."

"It just happened," and I told him about the druggies.

"Great school you got there."

"Public education at its best here in the end times of Y2K."

"Yeah, if that ain't a bunch o'... crap! That's why I don't wanna know about computers. More trouble 'n they're worth!"

"You're right: there's nothing to worry about. Y2K is all hype. You can party when it's 1999, and the world will still be alive."

"So what about the murder case?"

"Well, I have a confession about that."

He looked surprised and disbelieving.

"So your case is solved now?"

"No, it's more complicated, because the confession's from me," and I told him about breaking into the van. Mr. Stark's face became scolding and unpleasant.

"Look, kid, this game's gonna get ya into some real trouble 'n' that's a fact."

"I'm telling you about this, Mr. Stark, so you'll see that I don't believe it's a game." He just grunted and reached for his cigar, then remembered my objection from our last meeting.

"Last time you said you'd give me some pointers. So where would you point me about this: a male school janitor, around 30 years old, unmarried, probably a loner, who has a toolbox…with 2 stuffed toy bears in it?"

Frank Stark looked concerned. He went over to the window, opened it a little, and walked back to his desk.

"This janitor's your suspect, right?" he asked, while turning the pages of a yellow legal pad. This was hopeful: he had kept the notes from our first meeting.

"Yes," and then I described the van inside and out. He sat down and sighed, but didn't say anything.

"The bears seem… weird," I said. "The first thing I thought of was that they belonged to Aura Malper and to Anna, and that he took them as mementos of his crime, or as trophies."

"I guess that's possible. Any idea if these girls had a toy bear with 'em at school?"

"With Aura I have no idea. With Anna, well, I never saw one. But who knows what they might have carried in their bookbags."

"Wouldn't that be kind of unusual? I mean, for a high-school girl to be carrying around a toy bear? That's more for little girls in grade school, seems to me."

I had to admit it was unusual.

"But it's kind of unusual for a grown man, with a van full of beer cans and sunscreens of heavy metal rock groups, to have teddy bears in his toolbox."

He had to admit it was unusual.

"But, look, kid, by itself it really don't mean much at all."

"I know that. That's been the whole problem with this case. The few scraps of evidence I've been able to put together lead to this janitor, but they won't stand up in court."

"That's right. Ain't no crime to have a teddy bear in your toolbox."

"So what's the explanation?"

"Who knows? Maybe they are some sort o' trophy from the murder, like you said. Still… could be all kinds of other explanations," but he didn't offer any. Then he tapped his desk with a pencil and said:

"Let this guy alone."

"I can't. I've got to know if he's guilty."

"And what if he is? If he's dangerous, what're you gonna do against 'im?"

"I've got back-up. It wouldn't just be me against him."

"You think you got back-up, huh?" and he grunted and shook his head. "You're gonna back up, all right, back up into all kinds o' trouble for yourself and your friends."

"I started designing your website," I said, ignoring his warning. "I can have it on-line pretty soon. Won't cost you a thing." Then I nodded to the shelves of equipment. "When's the last time you had a partner on a case?"

"Doesn't happen much at all, just sometimes."

"Then you probably won't need those walkie-talkies for a while?"

Mr. Stark picked up his cigar and walked to the open window.

"I must be nuts," he said, and then motioned for me to take them.

"What's their range?" I asked.

"Don't know exactly any more, but I'd say it's good enough for you." After puffing smoke out the window he asked: "What're you up to with this 'back-up' you've got?"

"Two words: Plausible deniability," I said.

"What's that supposed to mean?"

"It means if you don't know what's going on, you can honestly deny being involved."

"Oh I know there's something goin' on!"

"But…you don't know what that something is!" I headed for the door and put the walkie-talkies in my book-bag. "Thanks for these. Don't worry: you'll get them back."

"Yeah, I just hope the police don't hand 'em to me!"

I took the bus home, ate monosyllables with my parents for supper, and then went to my room. The next thing I had to do was check on a few things with Abby. I found her number in the school's directory. She was not surprised to hear my voice, and expected the next step in Plan C.

"I need you to remember something very carefully. Don't make a snap judgment."

"Now what's going on?" she asked, and seemed very upset.

"I need you to remember if Anna carried any stuffed animals in her bookbag."

"Like what?"

"Just try to remember." I didn't want to plant any memories.

"Well, like, kind of, y' know? She had this keychain. There was a little Winnie the Pooh on it. Is that what you mean?"

No, wrong bear. Another dead end, at least so far.

"So what's going on with this big plan of yours?"

"It's on hold for a few days. But stay ready, just in case."

My next call went to Steve Cadosia, but he wasn't home. So I logically called my cousin Martika, but she wasn't home either. Of course that meant they were out together doing something…on a school night. I didn't want to speculate on what that "something" might be.

Since breaking into the van had been so easy, another "breaking and entering" episode began to form in my mind. I would need a techiesexual: that's a teenage boy who has almost completely transferred his hormones into mouse-clicks. There were a few in my classes, so I decided to call Seth, the most likely candidate.

But the first problem of course was how to explain to him what I wanted to do, without explaining to him what I wanted to do!

"Sure, you can download spyware off the Internet," he said. "I've got some myself, just for fun."

"I've heard about keystroke programs. Got something like that?"

"Yeah, I've got one that'll send you an e-mail with an entire record of what's been typed every day if you want."

"That would be perfect."

"Five bucks and you got a copy tomorrow."

"Okay," I said, wondering where I would get $5.00, outside of committing another crime by either going through my mother's purse or my father's pants. I was losing count of how many illegal things I had done. Suddenly an idea came to me: "How good are you at basic hacking?"

"I think I'm pretty good. Beyond basic," and he scoffed at the term.

"I've heard if you delete something on a computer, it's actually still there."

"Sure. The only way to really delete something is to smash the hard drive with a hammer, or put it through an MRI scanner, like something really magnetic. Everything that's been saved and deleted is still around, embedded somewhere, like it's asleep, you know, and you just got to know how to wake it up."

"Like the Prince waking up Sleeping Beauty."

"Huh?"

Seth was a true techiesexual. I told him I would meet him before Math class and pay him for the copy of the spyware. The next problem would be to get into Uncle Al's office and load the program into his computer. I was positive that anybody who hid a teddy bear in a toolbox is probably hiding something else deep in the heart of his desktop. The evidence of a crime was there: I just had to ferret it out. Warrants and other legal stuff didn't matter to me, and still don't. That's the advantage of not being a real detective with the police. The disadvantage is that I was doing technically illegal things. But when you're arrogant, you can ignore that. That's the advantage of being arrogant!

And then the phone rang. It was for me, a call from Anna's parents.

October 20

No time to write last night, as you will find out.

Anna's father introduced himself, along with his wife: they had a speaker-phone. They wanted me to stop by the next day to pick something up that belonged to me, which was impossible, since I had never visited Anna at home, and had given her absolutely nothing of mine at school. So yesterday afternoon I knocked on their door and introduced myself to Anna's mother. She was nervously smiling and nodding and babbling that she was so happy that I could stop by! I didn't see too much resemblance between her and Anna. Maybe their mouths were similar. I stepped into the hallway, and then she rushed away and started calling for her husband several times.

So this is where Anna lived: a large, old-fashioned house from the early 1900's. Lots of oak woodwork: a big staircase down the hall, high ceilings. A rich person's house back then: now it was the house of not-so-rich people. The old cliché: things change. Anna's father came down the steps and greeted me with the same amount of enthusiasm as his wife. He was short, a little plump, and his face was closer to Anna's than his wife's. They were in their 40's. He had an envelope in his hand, but pointed to the living room with it.

I noticed all the flowers first. No doubt potted plants from the funeral. And then I noticed something else that made me angry instantly.

"We don't know what to do with all the plants yet," said Anna's father, as he noticed my expression. "Margie wants to keep as many of them as possible, you know, for Anna, but all the stuffed animals, you know, I think we ought to just give them to a day-care center or a children's hospital or something like that."

"Yes," I said concealing my growing anger, "a children's hospital. I think Anna would like that." I said "would like" instead of "would have liked" to make it seem that Anna's presence was real.

And I kept staring at all the teddy bears. And I remembered the 2 toy bears coffined in that toolbox, one for Aura and one for Anna. And I could think of nothing else for several seconds but the monstrous evil in a murderer who takes a toy bear from the memorials for his victims as a souvenir! It didn't matter if neither girl carried a teddy bear around: their memorials and graves were piled high with them! And Uncle Al snatched one for Aura and then for Anna. No, I don't care what Mr. Stark thought: this was the easiest, most obvious explanation!

"Anyway, we were going through Anna's room, and thought you should have this," and he handed me the envelope. It was sealed and my name was on it.

"Anna mentioned you a few times. It's nice to know she had made a new friend at school."

I didn't bother him with my philosophical definition of "friend" and that I didn't know Anna well enough to qualify. During the pause he became uncomfortable and his voice started quivering.

"We just don't understand why Anna... you know, you know the circumstances, and we don't understand. Probably never will. I know my wife," and he nodded toward the upstairs, "no, she'll never understand this. To lose a child, bad enough, but to lose a child, our only child, our daughter, like this!" and his voice quivered to the point of cracking. I felt like crying too, but was able to counterbalance the feeling with my rage against Uncle Al.

"Anyway, if there's anything you can tell us…when you read this… or if you know… anything right now…"

So what do I say? That their daughter's death by suicide-or-accidental-drug-overdose was staged by the murderer of Aura Malper and Richard Laurenz, and that the guy was still pushing a broom at school, probably looking for his next victim? I already knew what the police would say to Anna's parents: that they had heard this story already, from me, and that none of the evidence fits it, that I must just be distraught and making things up out of grief, so I can "make sense" of it all.

And how exactly does it help them if I say their daughter was murdered? Isn't that kind of death just as senseless as a suicide or drug overdose?

"It's just a mystery to me too," I said. "You know, kids, teenagers, nothing bad can happen to us. No fear, no limits," and I tried to smile a little. "But yes, I understand. I don't know why Anna would've written a letter to me when we could easily just talk at school. But if there's anything here to… to help, I'll be sure to let you know."

Anna's mom never reappeared. I looked back at the house. Studies show that parents sometimes get divorced after the death of a child, especially in cases like this. No doubt Anna's parents are blaming themselves to some degree.

But only one person was to blame: I could feel it stronger than ever. The bus ride was something of a torture. I resisted the temptation to read the letter before I got home. There was something holy about it. I wanted the right kind of place to open it, and public transit was not the right kind of place. At home I went to my room and turned on a CD with Glenn Gould playing Bach's *Goldberg Variations*. Then I opened the letter.

"Dear Sam…" I looked at the envelope, and then looked at the first two words again: "Dear Sam…"

I am not Sam! What was happening here? Why is there a letter to "Sam" in an envelope with my name on it? "Mind-messing" was much too weak a term now for this mystery, and I kept squinting at the first two words. Here's what the rest of it says: I've changed some of it so you can't tell my gender. And no, I don't know why I keep that game going. Maybe now it's just a habit.

"Thanks for telling me that you know about the murder too! I don't know why… wouldn't tell me about you. …is kinda funny. … thinks… is a real detective or something. That's why I'm writing this to you, so …won't maybe see us talking at school. It helps to know I'm not all alone in this, but I'm just so scared all the time, and tired. I just want everything over. I can't do this any more much longer. When can you be the one that goes to the police, so I don't have to? Like you said, you can be the one that fainted and everything? Don't tell… about this, cuz that'll just spoil things, I think. Let me know when you're going! See ya!!! Anna."

Sam! Dear Sam! I was pacing in anger again, but not against Uncle Al! I remembered Sam acting like he was just finding out about Anna at her funeral! A Great Performance! He knew who she was! Why the act? And why did he contact her to begin with? And how did he know who she was?

The last question was easy: he spied on me! He saw me with Anna often enough, even when I thought nobody was around or watching us, to figure out she was the prime witness. So he goes behind my back and tells her that he's a witness too, that he knows the real story behind the murders, and that he's been working with me on the case. Why does he contact her? That's harder: maybe he wasn't satisfied with how I was handling things, and thought he could do better. That's the polite, charitable answer. The darker answer is attention: maybe Sam thought he could get some attention from Anna. They're both witnesses to a terrible crime, the hanging of Mr. Laurenz, and their lives are now connected forever. Yes, that's exactly what I was thinking! Sam saw an opportunity to turn Anna into an instant girlfriend, or even a lover! I already knew that I couldn't trust Sam. Maybe his "earwitness" story is true and maybe it isn't. Irrelevant: either way, he sees a chance to meet a girl, a vulnerable freshman girl, a girl on the edge of a roof on a 100-story building, and she's looking for somebody to talk her down. And my way, going to the police, is just the same in her mind as jumping off and ending it all. But then here comes Sir Sam, a quiet, sort of handsome junior, riding to the rescue with the idea that he will lie to the police and tell them that Anna's story is his own! Sam is an expert in lies and phony behavior: he could probably pull it off.

So why the act at the funeral? Why not just admit that he already had guessed, had already in fact discovered who she was? Was he that afraid of my reaction? Was I that intimidating? Or was something else going on?

And when did Anna write this letter? There were some familiar lyrics in it, about being tired, about wanting everything just to go away, and so on. She had used similar words to me that last day at school, when Uncle Al became the prime suspect. It could've been that night, or earlier. I thought and thought, but then gave up: knowing "when" was not the main question right now anyway.

No, I knew the main question! *Why is a letter to Sam in an envelope addressed to me?* Various explanations got scrambled in my head, and I sat down at my desk to sketch them out. First Explanation: there are two letters! At the same time Anna wrote this one to Sam, she wrote one to me. Maybe she explained what they were doing? No, because this letter says definitely not to tell me anything about their plan. Maybe she was making up a story of some sort to put me off the track. Maybe it was just a note about… who knows? But as she puts them in envelopes, they get switched. That means only thing: if this theory is right…

Sam has a letter to me in an envelope addressed to him! Or at least he will have one: maybe Anna's parents haven't contacted him yet, or they have, and he wasn't home, or hasn't gone over to pick it up yet.

I dialed Sam's number, hoping to talk to his little brother. I was in luck: Josh answered the phone. I was in double luck: Sam wasn't home then. Josh said he was at a store. That was just maybe triple luck: maybe Anna's parents hadn't called him yet to pick up his letter. I had to be discreet with Josh, and asked him if anybody called for Sam last night or today. Since the answer was no, I wondered if Sam had talked to anyone on the phone recently. Again the answer was no. So I left Josh with the message to have Sam call me.

Possibility: Anna's parents just haven't gotten around to calling Sam yet.

Possibility: Anna's parents haven't found the second letter yet.

Possibility: Anna already gave Sam the envelope with the wrong letter.

Possibility: there is no second letter meant for me but addressed to Sam.

This last possibility bugged me! It opened up two unlikely solutions: Anna didn't have time to write the letter to me, even though she addressed the envelopes first. But people almost always save the envelope for last. I know: it's *possible* Anna is in the .01% of letter writers who address the envelope first. The other unlikely solution is that she never had any intention of writing anything to me, but addresses the envelope to me through a Freudian slip. One part of her brain wants to keep their plan from me, but the other part wants to confess the secret, and that part squeezes my name from the tip of her pen.

Again I called Sam, but he still wasn't home. So I decided to check in with Emma. Not home: studying at the public library, according to her mother. Then I called Cousin Martika. Again not home: went to see a movie with Steve Cadosia. Seeing a movie during the week? Well, they are in love after all! Or at least that's what they think.

I stretched out on the bed and just listened to the Bach CD for a while. I stopped it and switched to Bob Seger for a change of pace. His song about teenage sexuality *Night Moves* came on, a completely irresponsible song, but who listens to the lyrics? It took me to a movie with the same title from the '70's with Gene Hackman that I had seen a year ago. I'm pretty sure the song had nothing to do with the movie. It's a detective story, about a simple missing-person case, but the case turns out to be extremely complex. I thought about it for a long time. I've even wondered if the title isn't a pun on Knight Moves, in chess, except the detective is playing a kind of alien chess, where the rules change with every move, and you can never know what the rules are. You might be making a good move or a bad move. You can't know at the time, but slowly you realize that you're losing the game, despite all your logic and hunches based on the past.

I admit it: I thought I was losing the game, and I didn't like it! The only way to stop losing the game was to become the one making the rules. I changed my mind about Plan A: if Emma got violent with him, too bad. I'd be around to stop anything too brutal. And so all 3 Plans should have a green light: A and B and C. It's time to unleash Emma *and* Allie *and* Abby in the Mother of All Stings! Uncle Al's new shave and haircut will prove his undoing. They can all tell him how great he looks now, and because of that girls will suddenly find him irresistible. He won't believe his good luck. Three more girls to kill! And maybe more!

I called Allie and told her the plan was on: she was to start tomorrow. Uncle Al needs her attention! I reminded her that this plan was for justice, justice for Aura and Anna and Mr. Laurenz. And she had to keep her mouth shut, especially to Lana, otherwise she would fungify the whole plan. Then I called Abby and gave her the green light: tomorrow she would attractively ask Uncle Al if she could join the work-crew. I suggested the morning work-crew, since that's where he could probably use somebody. After a few minutes the phone rang. Sam wanted to know why I called earlier. He sounded tired, nervous, and even a little skeptical when I told him what I was planning.

"You're gonna scare him off. You said so yourself," he objected.

"I've changed my mind. Maybe a good scare is what he needs, and then he'll make a mistake, a big one, and that'll be it."

"Is this 'cause o' what you saw in his van yesterday?"

"Don't worry about that. Anybody else call you tonight?"

"Uh no, why d'you need to know who's calling me?"

"Just making conversation."

"What? C'mon, what's wrong with you? You're getting really weird."

"I need you to get Uncle Al out of his office tomorrow afternoon, and make sure he leaves the door open."

"How'm I supposed to do that?" and there was anguish in his voice, as if I had just asked him to swim an ocean. But I had a new hard suit of armor on right now, and I didn't want to hear excuses.

"You'll smell a fire in a locked storage closet, or you'll tell him that there's a pipe leaking in a bathroom, you'll find a way to make him get up and leave and check on something far away from that office! And then you'll be sure to keep the door open so I can get in."

"So what're you gonna do?"

"Plausible deniability, Sam, plausible deniability."

"What's that mean?"

I weep for the future: doesn't anybody read anything? I sighed and said:

"It means don't ask what I'm planning to do."

Today school was too slow. Mr. Dunwoody either had no idea what he wanted to do in World Geography in First Period, or he was hung over from being drunk last night. He was going on about the World Bank and loans to the Third World, and was completely unaware that most had no idea what the Third, Second, or First Worlds are. I hoped they could interpret the meaning of the term "World Bank." But who knows?

Anyway, Mr. Dunwoody finally noticed that several students had passed out from acute dumbdom. Unable to understand anything, their brains shut down. So Mr. Dunwoody decided suddenly to back up and start from the beginning. Basic Economics 101 was now starting up.

"Now think, everybody!" A true call to arms! I wondered if he had been in the military: he really knew how to rally and inspire the troops! "What do you need to have an economy?"

Silence is golden, they say! Ours was beyond 24 karat! Eventually I raised my hand: "Things to buy and sell," I said politely.

"Great! Exactly right!" and he was much too happy with my response, which he then wrote on the board. "And then what will happen?"

Shh! Hear those crickets, guys? Hear the air from the noses pressed against the desks? I raised my hand again: "Nothing."

Mr. Dunwoody looked confused. "Uh, well, no, something *will* happen. Now think, what is it?"

"Nothing will happen," I continued, "until somebody decides they want what somebody else has."

He seemed willing to accept this as a rest stop on the road to the answer he wanted to hear: "Well, okay, but this buying and selling leads to something. What is it?"

"It doesn't have to lead to buying and selling," I objected. This was waking people up: I could be causing some fun. A few raised their heads, smacked their lips, and blearily opened their drug-red eyes.

"What else does it lead to?"

"Crime: he has something I want or need, so if I'm bigger and meaner, I'll just take it. Happens every day here in the cafeteria and out in the parking lot."

"That's the exception, not the rule. What's the basic rule I'm trying to get at here?" and he looked around the room with a pleading expression. The buzzing of the fluorescent lights became especially noticeable in the long pause. I raised my hand again. He sighed and nodded toward me.

"The basic rule of economics is: nothing is free."

"It is if you steal it!" came a laughing voice. Everyone was amazed: this was the voice of Jordy, a burn-out sitting in the back. I turned and said:

"No, the criminal will pay time in jail for his theft."

"What if he never gets caught?" he smirked.

"Then he pays with the energy and fear he uses not to get caught. Either way, he pays somehow. You know the cliché, crime doesn't pay. The criminal will pay, even if he isn't caught."

Lana looked at me with something odd going through her mind. I remembered her question after Anna's funeral: "What are you mixed up in?" And when I turned the same question around on her, her face had the same odd look in it as it did now. This was the face of the intelligent Lana. And it remained on her after class, when she signaled to me.

"What did you mean by that?"

"By what?"

"When you said the criminal will pay, even if he doesn't get caught?"

"Didn't you hear my explanation?" I said innocently.

"Yeah, yeah, but like…" and she seemed very indecisive, as if the Dark Side of Lana Lazybrain were fighting for control of her mind and tongue with the Bright Side of Lana Lightyear. "What's going on about Al?"

"You tell me."

"You said he murdered that girl Anna."

"No, I said the odds were pretty good that he murdered Anna, because he's a Grade A sleazeball."

"And I still don't know why you said that!"

"Just messing with your mind, girl, nothing else going on!"

"Somebody said you were almost run down in the parking lot."

"That's the dangerous life of a Narc, even if you're not a Narc! Bell's about to ring." I left quickly for Biology, but Lana's face stayed with me. She was afraid that I'll be doing something to Al. My comments on criminals paying, even if they're not caught, made her think of my accusation against him. I should never have made that comment to her at the funeral, now that we really are going to do something to him. In any case, I shrugged it off as unimportant.

Biology had a quiz on cell structure, something I learned about 2 years ago. At least there was no lab today after the lecture. Instead of going to Phys Ed I wanted to skip out so I could call Mr. Stark. After everyone had left the locker room, I went in and borrowed a long green coat, and put it in my bookbag. Then I went to phone Mr. Stark.

"Don't you ever leave that office?" I asked.

"I'm just about to, kid, so now what?"

"Did your contact get those license plate numbers?"

"Well, yeah and no, wait a minute," and I could hear papers being shuffled around. "The one car belongs to a William Clinton."

I had never heard a more criminal-sounding name in my life! And it meant that known druggie Jared Clinton was behind the wheel of the car that tried to pancake me.

"The other number didn't come up. You musta wrote it down wrong." He recited the number from Uncle Al's van exactly as I had written it. This was very odd: maybe I made a mistake. So I told Mr. Stark I would check the number again.

The doughnut guards would not be in the parking lot yet, since this was their hydrogenated-fat break. I put on the green coat and went out an exit in the rear by the gym, where my class was watching Mr. Hudson check the horse-racing guide in the newspaper. It took some searching but eventually I came across the Clinton Car, and with My Little Helper, who resembles needle-nosed pliers, a miracle occurred! Four flat tires on one car in under 30 seconds! Vigilante justice: the coolest thing ever! What a rush! Better than any drug!

Next I went to Uncle Al's van to check the license plate number again. No, the number was right, but there was a detail I had not seen. The license plate was for a truck. That explained why it probably didn't come up in the search. So I called Mr. Stark's office and left a message to check the number under truck license plates. I returned to the locker room, put the green coat back, and joined my class for the last 10 minutes of the period.

In the cafeteria I caught Sam and reminded him to be ready this afternoon. He seemed grimmer than usual, so I told him to relax. In a few weeks everything would be over. I also told him we would be following somebody again today after school. He looked less than enthusiastic, but I didn't care. I circled the cafeteria, found Emma Risley, and signaled to her. She followed me at a distance to the library.

"Remember that plan I told you about?" I asked.

"The whacked-out plan?"

"I've modified it. Instead of you confessing to Uncle Al, you'll get him to start thinking of you as maybe his next victim!"

"Oh… boy! That's a lot better plan!" Except "better" meant "even more whacked-out" in her tone. I looked at her intensely and hissed:

"I'm going to tell you something about the case that nobody else knows," which of course was not quite right, since Mr. Stark knew, but I figured he didn't count. I told her about the two teddy bars in Uncle Al's toolbox, most probably trophies from his killings, like antlers or an animal's head on the wall.

"God! So that's what it was! So that proves it, doesn't it? Just like we thought: he's guilty! He killed Aura and framed my uncle! And then he killed Anna!"

"Legally it proves nothing, but with Anna dead, it's the best thing we have."

She refused to listen: "It's over! Why else would he have something like that? Because he's the killer, just like we thought! You've solved the case!"

"No, only maybe!" I tried to slow her down. "None of this is evidence yet. That's why you need to ask him about joining the work-crew, especially morning work-crew. And for the best results, you might want to undo some of those top buttons of your blouse when you ask him. You know guys."

"Yeah, I know guys," and she dragged the last word through the gravel of disgust.

"And then keep coming on to him and see what he does. Somebody will always be around if things go too far. I've got some walkie-talkies now. You can put one in your purse so I can hear what's going on when you're with him. But take it slowly. Don't be obvious."

"You've got everything figured out, don't you?"

"I'm working on it."

Algebra was a blur, and so was History. Who can concentrate when you're in the middle of a big operation like this? I suddenly had to deal with 3 girls in a sting operation, an attack by zombies on speed (Hey! Great name for a rock group!), and a plan to hijack Uncle Al's hard drive to get some evidence.

In English we were told to write in our journals for most of the class, and then turn them in: the topic was based on the most over-rated book of the 1960's. That's right: *To Kill a Mockingbird*. It's amazing how the New Yuck East Coast establishment is a bunch of suckers for southern accents. Let's face it: this book sucks big ostrich eggs! Without the Gregory Peck movie nobody would ever read this. Thank heavens the author at least had the good sense not to write anything else.

Of course, if I put all that in my journal, Mr. Randolph would get depressed again. So I wrote a few nice things. Actually I ought to turn this journal in! That would really freak him out! Anyway, I committed another crime in this class, but it's all in the name of the investigation. Mr. Randolph has a large file holder where we are supposed to place our journals. As I slid the folders to replace mine, I noticed something that I could use.

Anna's journal was still in the holder. He had never taken it out, maybe as part of the "memorial" to Anna, or maybe he forgot about it. I instantly withdrew it and returned to my seat. Crime was really too easy these days, which is why I am not very worried about consequences right now. I felt I had a right to investigate Anna's journal: maybe there was a clue about the letter to Sam, although I doubted she would share such things with Mr. Randolph. Quickly I deposited the folder into my bookbag and opened up the short stories of Franz Kafka, which were closer to my life right now than *Mockingbird*.

I waited for Sam near his locker at the end of the day. He slowly came up through the crowd and looked unhappy.

"I don't like this," he said. "I don't think we need to do this."

"Of course we do. Anna: have you forgotten her? She's why we need to do this. Not to mention Aura and Mr. Laurenz!"

"Why not just let things, you know, work themselves out?"

"They are working themselves out."

He sighed. "So where's this 'crisis' gonna be?"

"Like I said, upstairs in a restroom there'll be a runaway toilet in about 2 minutes."

"How?"

"Through one of the greatest inventions in the history of humanity: chewing gum. Give me two minutes, then go down and report it to Uncle Al. And when you go in, put your bookbag down so that it blocks the door. That should keep it from locking when you leave with him."

I went upstairs and caused some perpetual flushing in no time. Then I went to the end of the building to a staircase that Uncle Al and Sam would definitely not be using on their way up. From a window on a landing I heard a commotion in the parking lot. Death threats and obscure obscenities floated gently through the afternoon air.

Downstairs I cautiously walked to the janitor's office, but stopped at a corner and listened for voices. There were a good number of other noises from boilers and pipes, but I didn't pick anything up. So I went around the corner, and was happy to find the door blocked by Sam's bookbag. Quickly my hands flew like a magician's: I flipped the disk from my pocket into the drive, loaded it, and then decided to check his Internet history. With luck I would find something incriminating there.

Nothing. And I mean *nothing* because the computer was not hooked up to the Internet! No connection at all! I looked for a phone line: nothing! This meant that the spyware was worthless, because it needed an Internet connection to send an e-mail report. But Mr. Laurenz supposedly sent his suicide note to the principal by e-mail! That was the story in all the reports: he typed a suicide note with a confession about stalking and killing Aura Malper on this computer...

And then I thought to myself: no, you idiot, not on this computer! This has to be a different one, *because* the police confiscated the *other one!* That's standard procedure! I was humbled and angry at myself. I stepped into the hall and checked for sounds. Nothing yet. What to do? I would need a wire to hook the computer into the school's Internet access, and then download and hide a browser. But why bother, if he can't surf the Net anyway? This whole plan was just a waste! The only possibility is that Uncle Al manually connects the computer with a phone line every time he wants to check the Internet. So I just decided to open up as many files as I could right then and there.

Work schedules! Nothing but work schedules! No games, no pictures, no documents: nothing but a spreadsheet with work schedules! I couldn't believe it. He did have a word processing program, but he had apparently never used it.

It was hard to believe that Uncle Al did not want his computer hooked up to the Internet. Maybe the administration didn't want it hooked up: but why? More likely: the school's computer technician didn't have the time yet to get that wire connected. No matter what the reason, the result was the same: there was nothing in the computer I could use.

Again I went out to the hallway and listened and then looked around. I was still safe. I looked down at Sam's bookbag, and on an impulse began checking through it. If I couldn't spy on Uncle Al, I would spy on Sam instead. He had lied to me enough that I decided I had a right to check through his stuff.

That kind of thinking is called rationalization: trying to transform something wrong into something right. Three lefts equal a right. I didn't bother thinking much about the morality of my search, because I was too shocked by what I found.

It was as mysterious as the teddy bears in Uncle Al's toolbox.

Why would Sam have this in his bookbag? And just to be sure I was seeing what I thought I was seeing, I lifted it out half-way. No doubt: it was the plastic cast from his broken-arm days, the one I saw in his room. Solution… solution… there was no solution! Except for stupid ones! He was planning on breaking his arm? He knows somebody who will break their arm? He knows somebody who has a broken arm, can't go to the hospital, and so needs his old cast?

Nothing was making *sense*!

I zipped his bookbag shut and left for the upstairs. On the way down were Sam and Uncle Al, the latter cursing most of the kids in the school as vandals wasting his time. Sam glanced at me, and I just nodded. Upstairs I headed for the library and marveled at the irony of a serial killer complaining about a little teenage vandalism.

A little teenage vandalism was about to bite me now. Lana happened to see me and ran up to me with wide eyes.

"You're in some deep do-do!" she said without actually saying "do-do." She whispered: "There's a guy in the parking lot screaming he's gonna kill the Narc. You know why he wants to kill you?"

"How do you know he means me?"

"God, c'mon, get serious! If he thinks you're the Narc, then you are!"

"He thinks that because he's a dealer and believes any rumor he hears about narcs in the school who are trying to catch him."

"You gotta watch your back."

"I always do. I have some back-up. Don't worry. I'm more prepared than you think for an attack," and I unzipped my bookbag somewhat and then put it on my back.

I left for the library and turned my thoughts back to Sam's arm-cast. How could I reveal to him that I had seen it? And would I be able to trust anything he told me? When he finally appeared, I asked:

"Do you have your Math book with you?"

He looked puzzled and said: "Well, yeah."

"I need to check on something that would be in it."

"But what did you find in Al's computer?" and he opened his bookbag, revealing the arm-cast.

"Nothing."

"You mean you're not telling me what you found."

"I mean I found nothing, zero, zilch, nothing." I hated using that cliché for emphasis, but Sam understood the truth. He pulled out his Math book, and then I pointed to the cast and said: "Why do you have that?"

"One of the football players I know kind of sprained his arm. I thought he could use it."

"Sprains are usually wrapped."

"Yeah, I just thought he could use some extra protection."

"So you must've broken your arm some time?"

"Yeah, well, not really broken, just a small fracture, when I thought I wanted to be in JROTC and was starting some of their training." He shrugged: "I lost interest and dropped out."

That sounded truthful, but I had become so suspicious, especially of Sam because of the letter fraud, that I still wasn't sure if I bought his story about the friend on the football team. I thought Sam didn't have any friends. Of course, he never said "friend" at all. "A football player I know" does not equal "friend" of course. Maybe Sam was trying to make the kid a friend through his thoughtfulness.

"So what happens now?" he asked.

"We wait to see what happens with The Plans. Keep your eyes and ears open when you're working this afternoon. But right now, I need you to go with me outside."

"Why?"

"I might be attacked by a drug-Nazi. If there are more than two, I'll need some help. Bring a broom. It might be useful."

Sam's eyes got real wide: "They're still after you?"

"We'll find out."

I deliberately walked out to the parking lot where drug-dealer Jared Clinton was waiting for a tow-truck for his quadriplegic car. Some other kids were standing around, but they were not necessarily his posse: most were just spectators. Now you would think that, if I'm a girl, he would not attack me in public. He'd wait to hurt me somewhere in private. The Sam-Factor muddies and confuses everything: whether I'm a girl or a boy, Clinton wouldn't want to attack me and risk a general brawl that would bring out the guards and any teachers. Because that could mean the discovery of any drugs he had on his person or in his car, which was his drug-store-on-wheels. So he was too smart to attack me right now, as I strolled by, smiled, and waved. He started walking toward me and screamed various curse words. Saliva soared through the air.

So I reached behind into my bookbag, pulled out my modified nunchuk, kicked him in the stomach, and snapped the nunchuk around his neck as he buckled over. This was all so unexpected that the small group did nothing: maybe they just stood there because I forced myself to smile the entire time.

"You see? Bad things happen when people try to run me over with their cars. Ever hear of karma? Why don't you answer? Oh, you can't breathe right now! A little joke for you! Anyway, karma means divine payback, but mine is faster. So right now, I'm going to say we're even. You stay away from me, and I'll let you breathe."

That's basically what I said. I might be exaggerating just a little. Anyway, after I unwrapped the nunchuk from his neck I gave him another stomach kick just to emphasize my seriousness, and then walked away and waved to the spectators. If I'm a boy, they were amazed. If I'm a girl, they were doubly amazed. So I won't tell you exactly how amazed they were.

"You're crazy!" said Sam.

"Spread the word."

"No, I mean, God, you brought a *weapon* to school! You could get expelled!"

"Who says nobody would do me a favor?"

"I'm serious! All those kids saw you with that thing!"

"What they saw was self-defense a la mode. Just without the whipped cream, but a whip might not be a bad idea."

I was jabbering jokes because I was just a little unnerved by the incident. (You can't call it a fight, more like a one-punch dive.) Yes, technically I had brought a weapon to school, but so had Clinton in the form of his car! I think that more than outweighs My Little Helper #2. I told Sam to go back to work and watch Uncle Al, especially when any of the girls in The Plans start their roles.

I sat in my room and thought. No music this afternoon: just the blood in my ears and random sounds from the neighbors. I sighed and zipped through my homework. Then I turned on a CD with Big-Band music from the '30s and '40's, Glenn Miller, the Dorsey Brothers, and so on. The sound quality wasn't bad. You always hear people say those were simpler times: how were the Depression and World War II simple? Weird how people think now and then.

Okay, I confess: I was avoiding something. Anna's file folder from English was in my bookbag. I wanted to look at it, and didn't want to. Her letter to Sam was on my desk. I read it again, wondering if I had missed anything. Eventually I would have to show this to Sam, and it would be another little unpleasant confrontation... for him! I put the letter back in the envelope, and then threw her file folder onto the desk.

I recognized journal assignments from back in August and September. Her grades were not bad. But then, right when Benny Goodman was sending his clarinet to the top of its capability, I began feeling a shock. The handwriting in the assignments!

The handwriting didn't match the handwriting in the letter!

Another fraud! And so far every time there is something phony in print, Sam is behind it! But why? And how?

October 22

I took yesterday and today off for various reasons: Mr. Jared Clinton, school pharmacist, might be looking for some karma of his own with some help from his pill posse. That's obvious, as is the other reason: Sam's fraud with the letter from Anna.

Assuming that my first hunch is right. I was already backing off from it: maybe I was being too hasty. The handwriting was different, but there could be other explanations for it. I don't mean trying to analyze it with graphology. Graphology is a false science. Anybody with any brains knows that. Just because some nice man in a white lab coat starts talking confidently about how he sees envy or pride in the way words slant or in the loops of letters doesn't mean he's knows a thing.

But there were differences, and sometimes big differences. What was true about analyzing handwriting is that it can show broad changes in a person. If you're under pressure, and in a hurry, your handwriting will not be the best. If you have time and are being thoughtful when you write, then the handwriting is neater. That should be obvious. I found some real scientific research on the Internet that showed changes when people become depressed. Anna was depressed, but she was depressed all the time since the murders.

So did Anna write the letter or not? Did Sam forge it somehow? If so, why? Just to get my attention again? Why didn't he admit that this forgery might show up, when I exposed his "Get off the case!" fraud? Maybe he was hoping it would never surface.

I was afraid I was missing something obvious, that I was again making a mistake.

I had to take a deep breath and think clearly again: there were just too many things floating around all at once. And I was losing confidence. One thing always helped: Pat Benatar's *Invincible*. And then back to Bach with *The Well-Tempered Clavier* for some well-tempered thought-cleaning.

After listening to this I called Frank Stark. No answer. I left a message on the answering machine. Probably out on a case, although marital cheating in the middle of the day seems a little unusual. Maybe it isn't: maybe that's when it happens most often. Then something came together: last night nobody I called was available either. Emma, Martika, Steve Cadosia, and Sam. Four juniors, all unavailable at the same time. I think that happened before.

Were they all together? Maybe Sam wasn't as lonely as he wanted me to believe! Was Sam going behind my back and planning something with the other 3? What would they be doing? (There was always one possible answer for Martika and Steve, although I didn't want to believe it.) Then I remembered the line in that letter: "… thinks… a real detective." She didn't like my ideas, and apparently neither did Sam. If the letter is real somehow, even with the non-matching handwriting, it means Anna and Sam were planning stuff behind my back. So it's no stretch now to believe the same thing is happening.

The question remains: what were they doing? Following Uncle Al? Planning their own investigation of him? This chewed my brain all day, and I kept going back to Sam's forgeries, Anna's journal, and the letter. It would be easier if the letter were printed on a dot-matrix printer! I kept looking back and forth and debating: yes, maybe Anna did write the letter. If she wrote it fast, maybe on her lap on the bus, that would account for the differences in handwriting.

So then the old question: where is my letter from Anna? Or was my name on the envelope a Freudian slip?

I got dressed and went to school on my bike. Miracle recovery. I pedaled fast and got there right before dismissal and looked for Sam near his locker. Instead Emma found me.

"You're in trouble."

"Why? Because I skipped today? My mom called me in sick."

"No, Clinton's telling everyone he's pressed charges against you, that he called the police and everything."

A teenage drug dealer getting the police on his side: these are the end times! In any case I didn't believe it.

"I tried calling you last night, but you weren't home."

"Yeah, I was out with my mom."

Okay, I thought to myself. Is that where she really was? The response seemed natural enough. If she were secretly out with Sam, Martika, and Steve Cadosia, she might have practiced this alibi. But maybe I was being too suspicious.

"So you probably want to know about what happened with that janitor?"

"Obviously!"

"Well, he said he couldn't use anybody. Didn't seem very friendly. He barely looked at me. He almost seemed annoyed that I was there. He was all business, working on an electric motor. And there's something else, too, that… I don't know."

"What?"

"Well, I was ready to believe he killed my uncle and everybody else, because of your story. But, now, I'm not so sure. I just didn't get a feeling that he's the one."

"He's a good actor. There have been some serial killers who have families and go to church every Sunday. But when they go on business trips, somebody dies."

Emma was not convinced. If Uncle Al turned her down, then Abby and Allie would not be hired either. So I wouldn't need to track them down right now for their reports. Uncle Al just sank my battleships.

I looked around for Sam in the basement by Uncle Al's office, which was dark. Other members of the work crew were waiting there, including Lana and her friends. One of the part-time janitors came by with a key for the supply room, and everyone took what they needed. Somebody asked where Al was. The man just shrugged and said he must be sick today.

Lana came up to me and said: "Where were you first period?"

"I was sick this morning, but I'm feeling better now. I'm looking for Sam Worcester."

"Wow, must be some sort o' virus goin' around or somethin'," said one of Lana's friends. "Sam's not here today either."

Lana looked at me with all sorts of questions in her face: it was one of her intelligent faces, and it made me uneasy, as if I had done something wrong. Of course I had done something wrong, a couple of times, but it was all in the name of the investigation. She went off with the work crew and didn't say anything.

I had a bad feeling come over me. Uncle Al and Sam both sick on the same day. The blood rushed into my ears and I actually heard a kind of roaring.

And then I could see it!!!

Sam, alone, confronts Uncle Al, and maybe even tells him that he saw everything, and that he's finally going to the police! He thinks he can handle Uncle Al physically, but he underestimates the man. Uncle Al has experience in killing teenagers! He strangles Sam. A fourth murder: but how will this one get explained? No, I thought to myself. You're imagining too much without any evidence! The simplest solution is that there really is "a virus going around" and that they just happen to be sick today. I chased the fantasy away.

****

Hours have gone by since I wrote all of that above. I thought I was done writing for today, but I'm not. My hands are shaking, and I don't know what I'm going to do! This is the worst day of my life! And it's all my own fault for being stupid and arrogant! Everything's ruined!

I was eating supper with my parents when the police came to the door.

They wanted to ask me some questions for an investigation. My parents were disbelieving, and spoke clichés you would hear in a bad T.V. show or movie. There must be some mistake! Our child can't be mixed up in a police investigation.

I felt like I was in a dream suddenly: Jared Clinton actually did file a complaint? I couldn't believe it! But I didn't use any clichés. The detective was wrinkled, very thin, and looked upset. I wondered if he was the one who had been on the cases at school, and that was why he seemed edgy.

Sam! My daydream had come all too true! They were here because Sam's body had been found! And with that thought the dream-like state became even deeper, and I suddenly couldn't think at all. This is how it is, I thought, when you are on your deathbed: you are helpless, and you can't think, and you just wait for the end to come, except you never see it coming, because you can't think, and so you just try to breathe one more time, without hope, without any future, and whatever is about to happen to you just happens. You have no control, no willpower to control: you are completely powerless.

The detective spoke in an uncomfortable voice:

"Your name came up in a murder investigation today."

My mother shrieked, and my father sat down suddenly and asked how that could be possible. The detective asked for patience.

"Do you know a private detective named Frank Stark?"

My parents must have felt that they were looking at an alien replacement for me when I said: "Yes." But I couldn't think of why Mr. Stark could be connected to Sam's murder. Or was Mr. Stark dead, murdered?

"Did you ask him to check on a license plate?"

"Yes."

"And why did you ask him to do this?"

I paused slightly and looked at my parents, but basically I was on auto-pilot. The detective had his hands inside my brain and could find anything he wanted.

"I was investigating the janitor at school. I had some evidence that he was responsible for all the murders this year."

"Mr. Stark said that would be your story." He paused and said: "You were involved in a fight at the high school, where you used some sort of a club on a boy named Jared Clinton?"

"Yes."

Again amazement and disbelief swept across my parents. I have to admit I was amazed too. This detective had found all sorts of things pretty quickly. But again I wondered what the connection could be with Sam's murder.

"But it was self-defense," I continued, and my voice was fading because all of a sudden I had a second bad feeling. "Clinton tried to run me down with his car, because he thinks I'm an undercover cop looking for drug dealers at the school."

My parents wanted to know why this was the first time they were hearing this, and began beating themselves up for not continuing with my home-schooling. But the detective was very focused and asked them not to interrupt.

"Can I see this club?" He opened his suitcase, cleared his throat, and took out gloves and a large plastic bag marked "Evidence." Wrapped in a cloud, I went to my room and started shaking. The second bad feeling was beginning to form words: *he thinks I killed Sam!* Uncle Al is going to win again! How-How-How did this happen? Uncle Al must have heard about the altercation, and thought he could get rid of Sam that way! But how did he even know that Sam was a threat? With me it was possible to understand why: I had been with Anna too openly.

So now the last witness of his original crime is dead, and it's being pinned on me.

I went back down stairs and tried not to let my arm shake or my voice quiver, because I thought shaking and quivering would make me seem guilty. The detective said nothing as he inspected the weapon and then dropped it into the bag.

"You weren't in school today according to their records."

"I was sick." And right then I felt sicker than ever before. I wondered if I would ever be able to eat again: my stomach had become a dense, sharp stone. And I would be awake for the rest of my life: how would I ever be able to sleep with Sam's murder on my head?

"But you were seen there at the end of the day."

"I was feeling a little better in the afternoon, so I decided to pick up my homework." That part was not untrue. But the detective had a way of looking at you, so that you wanted to tell him more. Rather absent-mindedly I added: "And I wanted to talk to Sam Worcester. But some kids said he was sick today too. I guess…I guess that wasn't really true now."

"He seemed pretty sick to me when I talked to him," said the detective.

My face must have started to melt into a puddle of chaos: my confusion was infinity squared.

"We've interviewed everyone on the school's janitorial staff, adults and students, about this case today. Sam Worcester brought your name up."

Finally! I thought. The police are going to arrest Uncle Al after all! He must have killed somebody today: if it wasn't Sam, then somebody else, and that's how the police followed the dots to me! This would be okay after all, except for whoever his latest victim was. It's too bad that somebody else had to die before Uncle Al could be caught.

"When we checked the victim's vehicle registration we saw that somebody had just brought up his record in the last day or so. That led us to Frank Stark, and he led us to you."

"The victim's vehicle?" I said weakly, in greater confusion than ever before, and yet, at the same time, my mind was assembling a pattern to bring order out of this chaos.

"The school janitor's body was found today. His name was Al Blasingame. The back of his head was beaten in."

He lifted the plastic bag with my nunchuk, and my parents gasped. My father began babbling about getting a lawyer. The detective said it was routine to check all possibilities.

"He seemed to be a nice guy. Had two little girls. They live in another state. He carried two of their teddy bears with him in his toolkit. Sentimental kind of guy, I guess."

I sat down quickly, because I was afraid I would faint. The toolbox, and the van: I'm an idiot!!!

My fingerprints are on it everywhere!

Yes, your honor, and ladies and gentlemen of the jury, the defendant is known to be violent at school, and nearly strangled a student with a nunchuk. Under the strange belief that the victim, Mr. Al Blasingame, was a serial killer, the defendant stalked the victim, even broke into his van and his office at school. The defendant tried to spy on Mr. Blasingame through the computer in his office. The defendant asked several girls to seduce the victim to get evidence against him. The defendant even tried to hire a private detective in a wild quest to convict Mr. Blasingame of murder. Obsessed with the belief that Mr. Blasingame was a murderer, frustrated when the police refused to believe such a fantasy, the defendant became a vigilante. Faking illness, the defendant skipped school, broke into the back of Mr. Blasingame's van a second time, and hid, waiting for the right moment to strike. The defendant brutally attacked the victim with this bludgeon in the morning, drove the van to an empty lot, and then returned home, thinking justice had been done.

Another case closed.

Conclusion

And so... yes, that was how the second notebook ended, so this is how Book Two of The Time Capsule Murders ends. Hamish and I were shocked by all of this too! I have to admit the last part of these writings made me a little queasy, especially when the narrator planned on using high-school girls to trap the janitor "Uncle Al," who was obviously innocent after all. What was the narrator thinking? What were they all thinking?

I wonder about Life and Death, just like anyone my age would wonder. This narrator makes me angry at times: the arrogance that he or she shows, as Death was hanging over this school. It was all just a game for this kid, and now he or she is may be responsible for the ultimate violence, the murder of the janitor, the prime suspect. Life and Death are not games: playing with people's minds and feelings all the time, making fun of them, doing things behind their backs.

Still, Hamish says I'm being unfair. The narrator was trying to find Anna's killer, even though the adults would not even consider the possibility that everything they believed was wrong. Obsessed with finding the killer, the narrator goes too far. Sometimes people begin to think the end justifies the means, the old idea that two wrongs really can make a right.

And now... obsessed with this story, even if it might be fiction, which I am still not sure about, obsessed with this story, even if it does cause us sleepless nights and strange dreams, which we do not understand, obsessed with this story, we have looked at the last journal with sighs of fear and with great curiosity. I feel like we're being allowed to look at a madman's torture chamber, a place filled with unspeakable pain so unimaginable that we squeeze our eyes shut… and yet… some invisible power opens one horrified eye to force us to gaze at ghastly, soul-screaming scenes. Yes, I have looked into the future and have read large portions of the final journal. In fact, I have already commenced the difficult task of transposing the handwritten pages. As I read them, I type and tremble, each stroke on the keyboard brings us closer to the truth – and it very well may be a truth I can't handle. As Hamish wrote at the beginning, I had a bit of a breakdown over putting this second journal together. Mostly because I know what's happening as I transfer handwriting up from the bloody pages, through my brain and onto through the tips of my fingers into my computer. Let's just say I make plenty of typos because my fingers are trembling.

In the end, the greatest mystery is how words on paper can cause such great emotions. These journals, after all, are just words collected together. That they could be relating something that happened – and that we may be uncovering the truth – that's what keeps me going. That the killer may still be out there and be aware of what we're doing is what keeps me up at nights. Dreams become nightmares when they continue into the unknown.

-- Hamish De'Lamet & Chandral Ramon

Lynchburg, 2010

The Time Capsule Murders:

Why Begins With W

Dial Emma For Murder

Hex High School

www.ingramcontent.com/pod-product-compliance
Lightning Source LLC
Chambersburg PA
CBHW051836170626
46807CB00003B/1204